KU-018-271

SPECIAL MESSAGE TO READERS

THE ULVERSCROFT FOUNDATION
(registered UK charity number 264873)

was established in 1972 to provide funds for research, diagnosis and treatment of eye diseases. Examples of major projects funded by the Ulverscroft Foundation are:-

- The Children's Eye Unit at Moorfields Eye Hospital, London
- The Ulverscroft Children's Eye Unit at Great Ormond Street Hospital for Sick Children
- Funding research into eye diseases and treatment at the Department of Ophthalmology, University of Leicester
- The Ulverscroft Vision Research Group, Institute of Child Health
- Twin operating theatres at the Western Ophthalmic Hospital, London
- The Chair of Ophthalmology at the Royal Australian College of Ophthalmologists

You can help further the work of the Foundation by making a donation or leaving a legacy. Every contribution is gratefully received. If you would like to help support the Foundation or require further information, please contact:

THE ULVERSCROFT FOUNDATION
The Green, Bradgate Road, Anstey
Leicester LE7 7FU, England
Tel: (0116) 236 4325
website: www.foundation.ulverscroft.com

RENDEZVOUS WITH A CORPSE

The wayward beauty who comes back to her old hometown to titillate her ex-boyfriend (now a married lawyer) and to blackmail her ex-husband is ripe bait for murder. And murder is just what she gets. Suspicion falls heaviest on the old flame: he was at the scene of the crime and out of his legal mind, befuddled by a number of potent cocktails. The police find his explanation incredible; but his wife, believing in his innocence, sets out to pursue an investigation of her own . . .

FLETCHER FLORA

RENDEZVOUS WITH A CORPSE

Complete and Unabridged

LINFORD
Leicester

First published in Great Britain

First Linford Edition
published 2017

A catalogue record for this book is available
from the British Library.

ISBN 978–1–4448–3166–5

1

It was a kind of natural conspiracy. Everything worked out just right to go wrong, and that's the way it went. I figured from the first to be a damn fool at last, and that's what I was.

It was late in the afternoon of a day that was in June, and I was in my office talking to Mrs. Roscoe Burdock, who wanted to divorce Mr. Roscoe Burdock, her husband, for beating the hell out of her while drunk. Mr. Burdock was, I mean. Drunk, that is. According, at least, to the testimony of Mrs. Burdock, which was probably not strictly unbiased. The truth of the matter was, I suspected, that Mr. and Mrs. Burdock were *both* drunk, which was a suspicion based soundly on precedent.

Mrs. Burdock is of no particular consequence in this account, except that there she was in my office, late in the afternoon of this particular day, and I wished she wasn't. I wished that she had never come, or would at least go away, because I was developing a feeling of sadness and loneliness that was already pretty bad and would keep on getting worse, because that was the kind of evening it was going to be.

You know the kind of evening I mean? It goes on and on, evening forever, under the softest kind of light drawn up from the edges of the world into the sky above the first transparent shadows of night, and there's a breeze that barely stirs the leaves of the trees, and in among the leaves are about a million God damn cicadas sawing away with their legs, or vibrating their wings, or doing whatever cicadas do to make the sad-sounding and lovely racket that they make. That's the kind of evening I mean, and it is not the kind in which someone like Mrs. Roscoe Burdock is welcome or wanted. It is the kind into which you withdraw alone to weep without tears, remembering every pretty girl you ever kissed or didn't kiss, and thinking with sorrow of all the things you haven't done that you will almost certainly never do, and of all the places you have never gone where you will surely never go. It is an adolescent kind of emotionalism, immune to reason. A man in its spell is in danger.

I was in its spell, or beginning to be, and in danger, although I didn't know it, and Mrs. Burdock was telling me how Roscoe had held her by the hair and belted her in the eye. She had the shiner to prove it, but I wasn't especially impressed.

'Roscoe's pretty impulsive when he's drunk,' I said.

'Roscoe,' Mrs. Burdock said, 'is a lousy bully and a bum.'

I leaned back and made a little tent of fingers over which I sighted through Venetian blinds at the neon sign of the Rexall drugstore on the corner across from the Merchant's Bank Building, in which I had, second floor front, my office. I avoided looking at Mrs. Burdock's face, which had been, the last time I looked, both belligerent and aggrieved, as well as oily and ugly, and did not meet my modest and flexible specifications of a pleasant sight.

'You're entitled to your opinion,' I said. 'I'm thinking, however, of the last time this happened. Perhaps you remember.'

'Of course I remember. How could I forget something that happened only last week? Every time the bum gets drunk, he takes a swing at me.' Mrs. Burdock paused, staring at me with sudden sour hostility, as if I had invaded her privacy. 'What I don't understand, though, is how you happen to know anything about that occasion. It was a private fight.'

'I wasn't referring to the last time Roscoe got violent,' I said. 'I was referring to the last time you wanted to get a divorce. After I had given your case considerable time and work, you and Roscoe kissed and made up and left me holding the bag.'

It crossed my mind that it had really been Roscoe who held the bag, but it didn't strike me as being funny, however true. I was far too sorrowful to think that anything was funny. Everything was sad. Everything was going or gone. It would soon be too late for anything, and the elegy of dreams would shortly be sung in the trees by a million sad cicadas.

'That was a mistake you can bet I won't make again,' Mrs. Burdock said.

'I further recall,' I said, 'that you called me a shyster and accused me of trying to break up the happy relationship between you and Roscoe for the sake of a dirty fee.'

'I was wrong,' Mrs. Burdock said, 'and I admit it.'

'A fee,' I said, 'no part of which I have ever collected.'

Mrs. Burdock quivered in her chair. I did not see her, but I felt her. She was probably offended by my lack of sensibility in considering anything so base as a fee when a crisis in human relations was in progress. After a few seconds, she grunted and stood up. I did not see her, but I heard her.

'It's plain you're trying to avoid taking my case,' she said, 'and so I had better get me another lawyer.'

'What I'm trying to avoid,' I said, 'is the charge of trifling with the holy union of a happy couple joined by God.'

'It pleases you to make fun of me,' she said with dignity, 'and what you are, after all, is the shyster I called you.'

I chose to ignore both indictments, the latter because it didn't logically follow, and the former because it wasn't true. Whatever my status as a lawyer, I took no pleasure in giving Mrs. Burdock the treatment, and I did it only to expedite her departure. To this extent, at least, it was effective, and my pleasure, what little there was, was derived solely from watching her massive stern clear the doorframe by the merest margins, larboard and starboard, on the way out.

I had risen at the last moment in a tardy concession to courtesy, and before I could sit down and take sight again on the Rexall sign across the street, I was distracted by the red head of Millie Morgan, which appeared in the doorway and came into the room. Millie is my secretary, and her head was followed, naturally, by the rest of her. The rest of Millie happens to be even more distracting than her head, especially when she takes dictation with her knees crossed, and the fact that my wife tolerates her amiably is less a commentary on my stability than on my wife's serene confidence in her own assets, which are, in fact, considerable.

'What was wrong with Mrs. Burdock?' Millie said.

'Roscoe belted her in the eyes.'

'I don't mean that. I mean when she came out just now. She looked as if you'd made improper advances or something.'

'Pleased and flattered, you mean?'

'Don't be absurd. Offended, I mean. Like a haughty hippo.'

'Do you think Mrs. Burdock would actually be offended if I were to make improper advances? There's a good chance, I think, that she might be receptive. Even enthusiastic.'

'That's because you're abnormally lewd and vain. Do you make salacious speculations about all your female clients?'

'Only when they're exceptionally seductive, like Mrs. Burdock. Of course these good lookers are often disappointing when you put them to the test. I'll let you know about Mrs. Burdock later. We have a date to go for a drive in the country tonight.'

'You'd better watch out. You're going to get sued someday.'

'That's all right. I know a good lawyer.'

'Do you? I don't. The only lawyer I know couldn't crack a case of beer.'

'In that case, you're fired. Go on home.'

'I'm not going home. I've got a date for cocktails and dinner with an engineer.'

'Have fun.'

I watched her go through the doorway, as I had watched Mrs. Burdock go before her, but there was quite a difference. My pleasure was differently incited, for one thing, and the larboard and starboard clearance was much greater, for another. When she was gone, I sat down and submitted again to the abortive sorrows of the incipient evening, the elegiac contemplation of going and gone, and I sat there alone for about twenty or thirty minutes, I think, before looking at my watch and seeing that it was almost five-thirty and time to be starting home. I got up and went through the outer office, a matter of half a dozen steps, and on into the hall. I slammed the door behind me and turned to try it, to see if the lock had caught or not, and there on the frosted glass of the door in neat little gold letters was a name, W. Gideon Jones, which was mine, and a designation, attorney-at-law, which was what I had become and what I was.

It seemed to me that an attorney-at-law was something a man might be if he didn't have the imagination or daring to be something else, and I stood there looking at the neat little gold letters and thinking of all the fine and exciting things I had never done and would never do because I was a picayune fellow who had lived all his life, time out for the university and a service hitch, in one small city of thirty thousand souls and a million cicadas. I might have gone to Florida and bought a boat and taken people deep sea fishing. I might have gone to Paris and lived on the Left Bank and had some Henry Miller experiences. I might have been a soldier of fortune in hot and gaudy tropic lands. At the very least, if I had to be a lawyer, I might have been, for God's sake, Perry Mason instead of Gideon Jones.

But there I was for a fact. Gideon Jones and no escaping it. Although it was a grim and unsatisfactory state of affairs, it was something that had to be accepted and lived with, and it occurred to me that acceptance might be a hell of a lot easier if I were to go over to the Kiowa Room, which was the cocktail lounge in the Hotel Carson, and have a couple of gimlets before going home. The more I thought about it, the more the Kiowa Room seemed like a good place to go, and drinking gimlets a good thing to do, and so I went there and did that, and I would have been better off, as it turned out, if I hadn't.

2

The gimlet was good, the bartender was taciturn, and I was grateful for both of these conditions. The bartender's name was Chauncy, and he had skin the color of Swiss chocolate surrounding large, limpid eyes that expressed mutely a legend of sorrow. On many occasions in the past we had settled issues of grave importance, Chauncy and I, but this evening he plainly preferred reflection to conversation, which suited me fine, and I think that he was probably anticipating the cicadas himself, and was maybe even listening to a private prelude by means of some kind of special sensual attunement peculiar to what he was.

I was sitting on a stool at the bar with my back to the room, and there were shadows in the glass behind the bar, the dim reflections of remote patrons, but I did not try to identify any of these shadows as people I knew who might want to make problems of themselves by being gregarious. I drank the gimlet unmolested and was well on with a second, supplied by Chauncy in response to a gesture, before someone spoke from behind my left shoulder into my left ear.

The voice came clearly from the distaff side of sex, and it contained a remarkable husky quality that I had heard before and remembered well, but at first I couldn't believe that I was hearing it now. It was the kind of voice that a woman sometimes acquires with a sore throat or from drinking far too much gin. You do not quickly forget this kind of voice under any circumstances whatever, and you do not forget it at all, even after seven years of silence, if you have heard it with all the nuances of tenderness and passion and sometimes anger.

'One of the nicest things about coming back to a place,' it said, 'is meeting old friends in general and some old friends in particular. Hello, old friend.'

I looked into the mirror and saw the face that went with the voice, and it was practically the same face that had gone

12

with it when I had last encountered them together. Seven years in passing will leave a trace here and a trace there on the best and most durable of faces, however, and this one was a little leaner than I remembered it, a little more posed and guarded against being caught unaware. Still, for all that, one of the loveliest faces, surely, in all the world, and one that I had never thought to see again. Part of gone. A passage in the evening elegy of cicadas. Part, although I didn't know it, of the natural conspiracy of a particular day.

I spun slowly, half a turn of the stool, and faced the face directly. Beth Webb was its name. I had loved it once, and it had loved me. It had said so, at least, although in the end it hadn't acted so.

'Well, for God's sake,' I said. 'Hello.'

'You look about the same,' Beth said. 'Hair, teeth, no glasses yet. Is everything really yours?'

'All mine. I wear glasses to read. You can hardly expect a man to survive seven years without deteriorating a little.'

'Has it been that long? Actually seven years?'

'Seven lean years. The period of famine. Wasn't there something like that in the Bible or somewhere?'

'Darling, I'm sorry. Has it been difficult for you?'

'Not at all. Everything has been fine.'

'Well, you mustn't sound too cheerful about it. I'll feel better if you suffered just a little. What's that you're drinking? It looks good.'

'It's called a gimlet, and it's made of gin and lime juice.'

'Is that all? Just gin and lime juice?'

'That's all. If you don't count the cucumber slice.'

'It doesn't sound quite as good as it looks. I'll have one with you, however, if you'll ask me.'

'Excuse me. Will you have a gimlet with me?'

'Yes, I will, thank you.'

I ordered one for her with a gesture to Chauncy, and another for myself with the same gesture, which made one more than I'd planned to have, and I carried both of them over to a little table where she had gone to sit while I was waiting. It was a very small table, and we accidentally touched knees for an instant under it, and I thought sadly that it had been a long time, seven lean years of famine, since I had touched her knee, either accidentally or on purpose, under a table or elsewhere. She was wearing a black dress with a narrow skirt, a sheath, and a tiny black hat on her pale blonde head, which was natural. She had always looked good in black, and she still did. My fingers had always itched for her when she wore it, and they still did. I had a drink of my third gimlet while she was having a drink of her first.

'How do you like the gimlet?' I said.

'Much better than I expected, I'm happy to say. It's remarkable how the lime juice disguises the gin.'

'Bear in mind that it's only disguised. It's still there, three to one.'

'That's quite a strong drink, isn't it? Do you think several of them would make me drunk?'

'It's possible. Even probable. It would depend on your tolerance for gin.'

'I think I would like getting drunk on

15

gimlets. Would you care to get drunk on gimlets with me?'

'Time was I'd have accepted with pleasure. Now I must beg to be excused. Sorry.'

'Don't apologize, please. I deserve your scorn. I may simply get drunk on gimlets all alone.'

'Do I detect a note of bitterness? Is it possible that the lean years have been difficult for you too?'

'Now good, now bad. One doesn't expect too much, darling. Tell me about yourself. What have you been doing all this time?'

'Routine stuff. Practicing law. Getting married.'

'I heard about that. It made me sad, and I wanted to cry.'

'I was weak. I should have mourned you in celibacy all my life.'

'That would have been romantic, but hardly called for. After all, I couldn't expect you to do what I was not willing to do myself.'

'True. Celibacy would not have suited you. Such a waste.'

'Thank you, darling. You made that abundantly clear, I remember, long ago. What is your wife like?'

'Small but potent. She has brown hair and nice legs and a warm heart. Her name is Sydnie, but I call her Sid. We were married three years ago.'

'She's lucky. You tell her I said she's lucky.'

'Cut it out, Beth. She's not lucky, but she's satisfied. So am I, and it's a nice arrangement.'

'I've tried and tried to remember her, but I can't. Did I know her?'

'No. She came here after you went away.'

'How convenient for you. You see how things work out, darling? It's a law of compensation or something.'

'Is that what it is?'

Was it? Going was still going, but gone had come back, and I thought it might have been the law of diminishing returns. I could hear the cicadas as plain as plain, all up and down the streets of town in a thousand tremulous trees.

'Darling,' she said, 'my gimlet is all gone.'

'They're very small and go quickly,' I said. 'Perhaps you'd like another.'

'I'll have another if you'll have another with me. Please do.'

'Well, I don't know. I've had three, which is one more than I intended, and if I have another it may lead to my doing what I said I wouldn't.'

'Getting drunk on them with me? What a charming prospect! As I recall, we frequently used to do things together impulsively that we hadn't really intended to do.'

'Yes, we did, didn't we? As I also recall.'

'Please do have another with me. Don't you want to?'

'Yes, I do, and I will. Damned if I won't.'

I went to the bar and got them and brought them back. I handed her a glass with a small bow, and our fingers touched. I sat down, and our knees touched.

'Why have you come back?' I said.

'Didn't I tell you? To meet old friends.'

'I know. Old friends in general and some old friends in particular. Am I general or particular?'

'How could you ask? Have you forgotten all our fervid moments?'

'I haven't forgotten. I just wasn't sure whether they were part of your general or particular treatment.'

'You mustn't be unkind, darling, even though I may deserve it. It would spoil all our beautiful memories and might even make me sorry that I came back and saw you and had these good gimlets with you. Don't you agree that our memories are beautiful?'

'I'm not so sure. Especially about the one of your rather impulsive marriage to Wilson Thatcher. Believing as I did, with some justification, that I was going to marry you myself, I was naturally puzzled and disappointed.'

'Did I ever say I would marry you? I can't recall that I did.'

'You're right. You didn't. There was no specific commitment. As I said, however, there was some justification for my belief. Including a couple of rehearsals of the feature attraction, and I don't mean the ceremony.'

'I said loved you, which was true, and I only tried to show it. I admit that it might have been natural under the circumstances to assume too much.'

'My error. My only excuse is that I was young and credulous at the time.'

'Surely you can understand why it was necessary for me to marry Wilson.'

'Oh, surely. All that money.'

'That's correct. It was the money that made me. Several millions of dollars is a serious temptation, you know. A girl can scarcely be blamed for yielding to it.'

'I don't blame you. I concede that your decision was sensible, if not essentially pure by romantic standards.'

'It really wasn't much of a decision. It was just something that sort of happened. We were out dancing at this place on the highway, Wilson and I, and he got pretty well loaded and wanted to make love, and I said I was saving it for the man I married, which was almost true, if not entirely, and he said, well, let's get married, then, and it simply seemed like too good an opportunity to pass up.'

'Thank you for the information. There's

nothing like a primary source in the study of ancient history. The rest, however, is a matter of record. So you got married by a justice of the peace, and so you went to California a week later, and Wilson became manager of the California branch of the Thatcher factory. Shirts and jeans for the general market. Uniforms made to order. I hope you were very happy.'

'Actually it wasn't so bad for a while, but it didn't last too long, as you know.'

'Three years, wasn't it?'

'Almost four. Wilson was unreasonable and demanding as a husband, but in the end he was quite agreeable.'

'So I heard. No nasty lawyers. No public hangings of the wash. Just a quiet settlement between the two of you, after which you went to Mexico for a divorce. I trust that the settlement was substantial.'

'Oh, it seemed like a great deal of money at the time, especially when Wilson might have been able to avoid giving me anything at all, but now it doesn't seem like so much as it did then, because it's almost all gone.'

'So soon? What the hell have you been

doing, honey? Playing the market or something?'

'No, no. Nothing like that. You know how it is when you are going different places and enjoying yourself. You become sort of careless about expenses and things.'

'What different places?'

'Places like Miami and Rio and Acapulco.'

'No, I don't know. I've never gone to those different places. Sometimes I go to Kansas City.'

'They're very expensive if you live well.'

'It's better to have lived and lost than never to have lived at all.'

It came out of me just like that, just a little differently from the way it had come out of Tennyson, and I thought it was clever, because of the gimlets mostly, and I waited for some sign of appreciation, but I didn't see any. I tried to remember what particular piece of Tennyson the line was from, and pretty soon I remembered that it was from *In Memoriam*, and I thought that it was appropriate, considering everything else, that it happened to be. In memoriam of Gideon Jones. In memoriam of Beth Webb. Beth Webb Thatcher. In memoriam of going and gone and never, never.

'You'll find things cheaper here,' I said.

'I don't plan to stay, darling. Only a day or two. The truth is, I really came to see Wilson. I learned that he had moved back here to take charge of the main factory, and I thought he might be willing to give me some more money. He has plenty, of course, and wouldn't miss a little more.'

'Have you also learned that he's married again?'

'Yes. Marriage is the perfect estate for Wilson. It gives him someone to bully.'

'Don't you think it's possible that his wife may object to his giving money to an ex-wife with no legal claim to it?'

'So far as that goes, Wilson himself may object a little.' She laid an index finger alongside her nose and looked at me with a sly and intimate expression. 'In connection with his wife, it will be necessary to practice a certain amount of deception.'

She drank the last of her second gimlet,

and I drank the last of my fourth, and it occurred to me that there were probably quite a few people in the lounge who knew me, and some who would remember Beth, and of these there would certainly be a percentage who would recall the brief bit of pre-Thatcher history in which we were involved together. This, I knew, could be the stuff of gossip, if not of scandal, a meaty conversation piece for social gatherings, and I began to get a notion that I'd better get the hell out of there, but I didn't want to go. What I wanted to do was stay. I had recovered a bit of gone in an hour of going, and I wanted to keep it until the last gimlet. Not that I was filled with derring-do, a rash readiness to sacrifice all for gin and old love. I was only sad. I was merely filled with aches and pains and cicada sounds. I wanted a kiss for auld lang syne and a last goodbye to what would never be.

I thought of my position in the community, and it made no difference. I thought of my duty as a husband, and I thought to hell with it. Then I thought of her to whom the duty was owed, sweet Sid in short shorts probably this instant broiling rock lobster tails or sirloin strips on the charcoal grill on the back terrace at home, a sad husband's haven deep among the singing trees of Hoolihan's Addition, fine homes on easy terms with practically nothing down, and this thought made a difference not lightly dismissed, or not dismissed at all, for the call to Sid was not merely the call to duty, odious word, but the call to pleasure and later love.

One clear clarion call, I thought.

Tennyson again, for God's sake, I thought.

'I've got to get the hell home,' I said.

'Do you, darling? How too bad. I was hoping we could have another gimlet. Why can't we?'

'Because, in my case, another gimlet is a myth. There couldn't possibly be such a thing as another gimlet. There could only be gimlet upon gimlet, ad infinitum in an eternal night. Then, contradictory though it may seem, there would be tomorrow. It is the prospect of that gray tomorrow which compels me to excuse myself tonight.'

'Perhaps tonight would be worth it. Perhaps, after tonight, all your tomorrows wouldn't matter.'

'Is that an invitation?'

'Yes, darling.'

'RSVP?'

'Yes, darling. In English.'

I stood up and looked down at her, and there she was, looking up, in her black sheath with her little black hat on her pale hair and one sheer nylon knee on top of the other. It was a time of trial, I mean, and I was a long way from feeling full of beans and certitude and holy resolution.

What kept me clean for the moment, I think, was only a curious lassitude.

Smiling, she lifted her glass to her lips, but the glass was empty. The gimlet was gone, all gone, and I was going.

'Mr. Gideon Jones begs to be excused,' I said. 'Thank you so much.'

She smiled and shrugged and set down the empty glass.

'No matter, darling. Tell me goodbye and run along home.'

'I've already told you goodbye. Seven years ago.'

This was the gimlets talking again, but I thought it was a perfect exit line, spoken with restraint and salvaged dignity, and so I turned and walked away before I could say something else to spoil it, and there by herself at a table near the door was one of the ones who did indeed know me and Beth and our brief bit of pre-Thatcher history. Her name was Sara Pike, thirty and thin and slightly sour, and she was watching me with that carefully composed expression which can somehow be more of an indictment than a salvo by a Savonarola or even a Billy Graham. There were several packages on the table in front of her, surrounding something with a cherry floating in it, and she had obviously stopped in for a drink after shopping before going home.

She smiled at me, but she didn't mean it. She nodded and said hello, and I said hello right back with a composure that was, I hoped, equal to hers.

'Isn't that Beth Thatcher you were talking with?' she said.

'Yes,' I said. 'It's Beth.'

'How nice to see her after all this time. She looks hardly a day older, does she?'

'That's because she's been living well in different places like Miami and Rio and Acapulco.'

'Really? I must go over and speak to her.'

'You do that. I'm sure she'd be delighted.'

I considered that I'd handled that minor incident with admirable deftness too, and there was an element of pride in my sadness and sense of loss as I hit the street and headed home. In fair weather, for the sake of exercise, I make a habit of walking. This morning I had walked to town from home, and now I walked home from town. It was quite a way and took quite a while. It was pretty late when I got there.

3

I went in the front door and through the house and out the back door, and there on the little flagstone terrace was Sid. The sun was down, but there was still plenty of light left to last another hour, and Sid was standing there in this late, soft light in her short shorts with her back to me.

She was intently watching the cherry-hearted bits of charcoal in the grill, and on the round rack above the coals, pushed back to the perimeter of the rising heat, were four small lobster tails with skewers stuck through them lengthwise to keep them from curling up. There was also a little pan full of drawn butter, in which the tails were to be dipped when eaten.

In short shorts, approached from behind, Sid is delectable, to say the least, and my normal reaction to her, when I am the one approaching, is organic and emphatic, but in this instance the reaction was somewhat qualified by a kind of subtle pathos that may have been more a subjective matter of me and gin than any impression she actually gave. Anyhow, she looked *deserted* with her broiled tails and drawn butter, as if she had waited and waited for someone to come, which was true, and was now waiting on and on in the knowledge that no one ever would, which was not. The cicadas were raising hell in an oak, and I felt like a son of a bitch.

Crossing the terrace to where she was, I exercised a husband's prerogative and took a mild liberty with the near half of her compact bottom. She turned her head and looked up at me without speaking, and I kissed her, and we decided to hold the kiss for a while. Then she sighed and leaned against me, and I could hear her sniff.

'Where the hell have you been?' she said.

'I stopped in the Kiowa Room and had a couple of drinks.'

'They must have been big ones, the time they took.'

'Not so big. As a matter of fact, I had four.'

'The thing I like best about you, sugar, excepting a talent or two that I'm too proper to mention, is that you tell the truth under only the slightest duress. You smell like a gin mill.'

'I drank gimlets. Gimlets are made of gin.'

'I know, sugar. And lime juice and a slice of cucumber. You taste like gin too. I love gin kisses. Will you give me another?'

I gave it to her, and we held it again between us, and she raised herself on her toes to get closer to it.

'I was wishing you were dead,' she said, 'but I take it back.'

'That's all right. It would be a nice evening for dying if you didn't have to stay dead tomorrow.'

'I always wish you were dead when you make me feel like a wife. Sometimes I curse you a little as well.'

'Don't you like being a wife?'

'I don't mind *being* one. I just don't like *feeling* like one.'

'What *do* you like to feel like?'

'I like just now, for one thing. When you were kissing and petting me.'

'You're in luck. The two conditions you have mentioned are likely to recur frequently.'

'Well, I'm pleased to acknowledge that they have in the past, and so I'm naturally hopeful that they will continue to do so in the future.'

'Would you like me to kiss you again this very moment?'

'I'd like for you to, but I don't think you'd better. The late time made me pretty excited, and we might never get around to having dinner if you did it again.'

'I'll make a note of that. Not that a note will be necessary, of course. I see that you've been broiling rock lobster tails.'

'Yes. When you came, I was just wondering what the hell to do with them. They've been done for ages and are surely too tough to eat.'

'Let's try. It'll be a challenge.'

'There's a salad and a bottle of white Burgundy in the refrigerator, but I don't suppose it would be a good idea for you to drink the Burgundy on top of all that gin.'

'Now that you've mentioned it, I insist upon the Burgundy. What's so unthinkable, I'd like to know, about drinking gin and wine? Aren't you aware that Martinis, surely among the most commonly consumed of all cocktails, are a mixture of gin and wine?'

'That's true, isn't it? Vermouth is wine, and you mix it with gin to make a Martini. Isn't it odd that I'd never thought of that?'

'A very little bit, however. The vermouth in a Martini, properly proportioned, is just barely there.'

'Well, this is just a little bottle of white Burgundy, and so I guess it will be all right for you to drink half of it after all. We can eat out here, if you want to. There's still enough light, and the table's all set.'

'I want to. I'll take up the tails while you're getting the salad and the white Burgundy.'

She went across the terrace and into

the kitchen, and I went over to the glass and wrought iron terrace table, with two places set, and got the two plates and carried them back to the charcoal grill. I put a pair of tails on each plate and returned with them to the table. Then I went back again to the grill and put on a padded glove and got the pan of drawn butter. I was pouring the butter with a careful eye to equality into two little pots, one by each plate, when Sid came out with the salad and the wine. We sat down together at the table, and she began to transfer the salad with a big wooden spoon and fork from a large bowl to two smaller bowls, while I began to pour the wine.

The wine was a good domestic brand from a vineyard in California. It was chilled just right. The rock lobster tails were slightly tough from overcooking, thanks to me, but they were good, nevertheless, because, after all, how tough can a lobster tail get?

'Did you see anyone we know at the Kiowa Room?' she said.

'I saw Sara Pike,' I said.

'Was she the only one?'

'Yes.'

This was true, strictly speaking, for Sid had never seen Beth and didn't know her, and she had used first person plural, not second singular, which gave me an out. That is, it gave me a chance to be evasive, a God damn sneak, and so, after feeling for a few seconds like a God damn sneak, I took a swallow of good domestic white Burgundy from California and came clean.

'I saw someone I used to know,' I said. 'Before you and I met. Beth Thatcher. Used to be Beth Webb. She was a girl around town.'

Sid dipped a bite of tail into her little butter pot and popped it into her mouth. Chewing, she stared past me across the backyard into the gathering darkness beneath the oak, and she seemed suddenly to be listening intently to all the sounds around us.

'I've heard about her,' she said.

'To tell the truth, we went together for a while.'

'That's one of the things I heard.'

'She married Wilson Thatcher and went out to California with him. Later they were divorced, and he came back without her when he took over the local factory. Now she's in town for a day or two, and I had a couple of drinks with her.'

'Are you back to a couple again? I thought it was four.'

'I had two before she came in.'

'Oh, well, that's all right, then. Two drinks with an old girlfriend are permissible, even if it means keeping me waiting and waiting while the God damn lobster tails get tougher and tougher, but four would be too many and not permissible at all.'

'She asked me to buy her a drink, so what the hell could I do? I had to be courteous, at least.'

'Of course you did, sugar, and I admire you tremendously for it. If you keep practicing, you may even become courteous enough to make a reasonable effort to come to dinner on time and things like that.'

'Oh, hell. I can see that I made a mistake in telling you about it.'

'Do you think so? Why? Do you think I'm being unreasonable or something? I simply can't understand you.'

'All I can say is, if you don't want to be *treated* like wife, you'd better try not to *act* like one.'

'Now, why in hell would you make a remark like that? Have I said a single thing to justify your calling me a dirty name? All I did, in connection with the number of gimlets you had with your old girlfriend, to point out calmly that enough is enough and too much is too God damn much. That's all.'

'Oh, cut it out, Sid. Please do. I'm sorry I was late, and I'm sorry I had the damn drinks with Beth.'

'Well, now that you're properly contrite, I may as well admit that I may have been a little unreasonable about it. I think it was mostly because you came directly home afterward and covered me with gin kisses. I got the impression that you were trifling with my affections.'

'It wasn't your affections I was trifling with. You wait a while until it's a little darker, and I'll show you some trifling you'll remember.'

'That would be nice, sugar, and I'm all over prickly just thinking about it, but I can't possibly stay for it.'

'Can't stay? Why not?'

'Because I have to go over to Rose Pogue's for a conference. She and I are conducting the next session of our discussion group, you know, and tonight is absolutely the last chance we'll have to get together and plan things. What we're discussing now is the great religions of the world, and Rose and I are having Zoroaster.'

'Why do you have to have a conference? Couldn't you each just take a part and plan it by yourselves?'

'No, no, sugar. Not possibly. We need to talk things over.'

'Well, if you must have a conference, why must it be so late? Don't you realize that it's already eight-thirty?'

'Honest to God?' Sid jumped up and tugged at the bottoms of her short shorts. 'Sugar, I simply must take a shower and dress and run. Would you mind too much clearing away the things? There are only a few, and you can simply put them in the sink and leave them.'

'You've eaten only one of your tails.'

'You may eat the other, if you wish. They're such little tails, I'm sure you can eat three easily. You may also drink all the rest of the wine.'

She went inside, and I sat there and finished the white Burgundy, but not the fourth tail. It was pretty dark now, and the moon and a mess of stars were getting bright in the sky. A mosquito began buzzing around my head. I made a couple of passes at it, but it wouldn't go away, and after a minute or two I got up and cleared the table and carried the things into the kitchen. I left the things in the sink, as Sid had suggested, and went upstairs.

Sid was out of the shower but not yet out of the bathroom. I sat down on the edge of the bed in our room and waited for her to come out. Pretty soon she did, as brown and lustrous as a polished acorn, and walked over to the closet and took down a sleeveless dress, pale yellow cotton that she was going to wear.

'Stay here, Sid,' I said. 'Please do.'

'Sugar, I can't possibly. Rose is waiting for me, and it's the last time we'll have to get ready for Zoroaster.'

'To hell with Rose and Zoroaster.'

'You mustn't talk like that, sugar. Zoroaster was a god once, even though no one believes in him anymore, and it's sacrilegious to curse him.'

She slipped the pale yellow dress over her head. I watched with regret as the nut-brown body disappeared, and I wished there was time to bring it back, but there wasn't, because of Rose and Zoroaster and the discussion group, and I felt bitter about this, somehow deprived, and I was getting lonely again.

'Sugar,' she said, 'please zip me up in back.'

She backed up to me, and I zipped her up, and she walked over to her dressing table and began to brush her short brown hair with quick strokes.

'Did you clear the table?' she said.

'Yes. I put the things in the sink.'

'Did you finish the wine and the tails?'

'I finished the wine, but not the tails. One was left.'

'You had better put it in the refrigerator, then.' She put the brush on the dressing table and shoved her feet into white flats and came over and sat down on my lap.

'Sugar, I'm sorry to run. Really I am. What will you do while I'm gone?'

'I don't know. Maybe read. Maybe listen to music.'

'You can think about when I get home. We'll have an interesting time if you like.'

'How long will you be gone?'

'It's hard to tell. Quite a while, I imagine. You know how Rose is about things. She insists upon considering every little detail that might or might not be important.'

'Try to be back soon,' I said.

She kissed me then, still perched on my lap, and I began to hope as the kiss went on that I might have my own way after all, but she finally pulled away just short of disintegration, and stood up, and smoothed her pale yellow skirt over her nut-brown hips.

'You keep thinking about later,' she said, 'and so will I.'

'All right,' I said. 'Have fun with Zoroaster.'

She went out, and I watched her. Slim brown legs below the yellow skirt. Bare brown arms and slender brown neck bearing erectly her proud brown head. I could hear her going down the stairs. I heard the screen door slam.

4

Well, she was gone.

She had deserted me without appreciable concern just when I was full of vague apprehensions and sorrows, to say nothing of gin and white Burgundy and lobster tails, and was peculiarly susceptible as a consequence to all sorts of idiocies.

What I thought was, if a man can't compete with Rose Pogue and Zoroaster, what a hell of a man he is. That's what I thought.

I had wanted her to stay, and she had refused, in spite of leers and suggestions and gin kisses, and even if I had ordered her to stay, no foolishness about it, she would certainly have refused and gone anyhow.

If you are looking for someone with a little authority, I thought, I have as little as anyone.

That wasn't original. I had read it on

one of these little signs that men buy for their desks. These little signs are supposed to be funny and make you laugh, but I wasn't unused. I was sad and lonely and at odds ends. I got up from the bed, where I was still sitting after being kissed and deserted.

I went downstairs and washed and dried all the things I had left in the sink. I put the things away in proper places and went out onto the back terrace and looked up at the moon and the mess of stars. They were bright and near now, but not so near as the cherry hearts of charcoal glowing through ash in the grill. I sat down in a canvas sling chair and smoked three cigarettes, which helped to keep the mosquitoes away, and then I went back inside and found a bottle of gin and made a batch of gimlets with Rose's lime juice, leaving out the cucumber slices, which are only decoration anyhow, and on into the living room, carrying a gimlet in a glass, and turned on a light.

I thought I might as well listen to some music, and so I went over to the record cabinet and began looking through the collection of records to see what I could find that would seem appropriate to the kind of night it was and the kind of mood I was in.

I am ordinarily a Haydn man, and will choose something by Haydn seven times out of ten, but tonight old Papa struck me as being a little too God damn cheerful, and so I looked through the records until I came to 'Death and Transfiguration,' by Richard Strauss, who was a good composer too, and I knew at once that this was exactly it.

I put the record on the player and sat down to listen and drink the gimlet. I remember reading in the *Autobiography of Benvenuto Cellini* about how old Benvenuto went down from Florence to Naples with this certain character he knew, and afterward he said he'd never go anywhere with him again, because he was the kind of character who constantly keeps your guts in a saucepan. At least this was how it came out in translation, and I thought that it was a fine expression for a particular feeling, and this is the feeling you get when you really listen to 'Death and Transfiguration' by Richard Strauss, especially on a night like this in a mood like mine. I drank two gimlets while listening, and then I started the record again and poured another gimlet, and I was drinking the third gimlet and listening to the largo, the very first part of the piece, when the phone began to ring in the hall.

I went out into the hall and answered it, and a voice said, 'Is that you, Gid?' It was a voice you would instantly know if you had ever heard it before, which I had, and the last time I'd heard it, after seven years, was that very afternoon in the Kiowa Room. I had been trying not to think of Beth, and I had been doing pretty well at it, all in all, especially when Sid had been around as a distraction, but now Sid was gone, lost temporarily to Rose Pogue and Zoroaster, and Beth's unforgettable voice had just spoken softly into my ear over a long wire, and for a moment it was just like back there before the lean years, and I had the same sharp, poignant feeling that I used to have then.

What had Beth said? Hadn't she asked if it was me?

'Yes,' I said, 'it is.'

'I'm so glad you're home, darling. What are you doing?'

'I'm drinking gimlets and listening to 'Death and Transfiguration.''

'Still drinking gimlets?'

'Not still. Again. I took time out to drink a bottle of white Burgundy.'

'Aren't you afraid of becoming drunk?'

'Not at all. It's possible and even probable that drunk is what I'll become, but I'm not in the least afraid of it. In fact, I'm cultivating it.'

'What did you say you were listening to?'

' 'Death and Transfiguration.' '

'Is that the name of a song?'

'A tone poem. By Richard Strauss.'

'Is that what I hear in the background?'

'Quite likely.'

'It sounds very gloomy, I must say.'

'If it didn't sound gloomy, I wouldn't be playing it.'

'Darling, are you unhappy?'

'I am. I'm full of gin and sorrow.'

'That's too bad. I'm sorry.'

'Be sorry about the sorrow, if you please, but not about the gin.'

'I believe you are *already* drunk.'

'That's a shrewd diagnosis, honey. You may be right.'

'Is Sid there?'

'No, Sid is not here. Sid's gone. Sid is off discussing Zoroaster with Rose Pogue.'

'Really? A thing like that can go on forever with Rose.'

'True. Rose is an exceptionally gregarious intellectual type. Windy is what she is.'

'Are you all alone?'

'Yes. All alone by the telephone. That's from a song by Irving Berlin, who is a composer somewhat inferior to Strauss.'

'I'm all alone too, darling. Couldn't we get together?'

'We could, indeed, but I don't think it would be wise.'

'We could be very discreet about it.'

'Discretion is fine in theory, but in this town difficult in practice. Surely you remember that.'

'Oh, come on, darling. Don't be such

a coward. Don't you want to see me again?'

'Yes, I do, and I'll not deny it. I might even want to kiss you a few times and tell you the proper goodbye that I've never had the chance to tell you.'

'Darling, I wish you would. I must go away again tomorrow, and I've been thinking about it ever since you left me this afternoon, and I simply can't bear to think any more about going without seeing you again first. Please come.'

'Come where?'

'Well, I'm staying at the hotel, of course, but I don't think you'd better come here. Do you remember Dreamer's Park?'

'Certainly. How can you ask? We stopped there now and again in the past to do a little necking in the old bandstand.'

'That's exactly the place, darling. Wouldn't it be exciting to meet in the old bandstand again? Like old times. I'll meet you there if you'll come. Will you?'

'Yes, I will.'

'In half an hour?'

'I'll have to walk. It may take a little longer.'

'As soon as possible, darling. Please hurry.'

She hung up, and I did too, and if you are thinking that I was a damn fool, I won't argue the point, but I would like to say at least that circumstances were extenuating, and everything, as you can see, was still working just right to come out all wrong in an afternoon and an evening and a night that were filled with the nostalgia and idiocy of going and gone. In my opinion, so far as I was involved, that damn Rose Pogue and Zoroaster were as much to blame as anyone else.

'Death and Transfiguration' was out of the largo and into the allegro. I went over to the player and turned the reject dial, and the arm lifted, and the music stopped.

Carrying the glass my gimlet had been in, I returned to the kitchen and found a little gimlet left that it seemed a shame to waste, and so I poured what was left into my glass and drank it. While I was drinking it, I closed and locked the back door, and after it was drunk I turned out the light and went out of the house the front way, and all this time I was trying to do just the opposite of what I had been trying to do all evening earlier.

I was trying to think only of Beth and not at all of Sid, instead of Sid only and not at all of Beth, but this did not work perfectly, of course, or even very well, for Sid is not the kind of person you can just quit thinking of in an instant, even for someone like Beth.

Nevertheless, I kept trying, because I knew that Sid would not exactly approve of what I was doing, not, in fact, by a damn sight, and the truth was, I didn't exactly approve of what I was doing myself, although I wanted to do it and was still feeling a little of the old ache for Beth that seven years and Sid had not quite cured.

'What the hell!' I said to myself in my mind. 'I am only innocently going to see an old girl for old time's sake.'

'Like hell you are!' Sid said in my mind to me. 'You are going to see an old girl for

51

tonight's sake, and not so damn innocently, either, if you ask me.'

I hadn't asked her, but she kept telling me, and I kept trying not to listen and to think of Beth only as I walked along. Dreamer's Park was quite a long walk away, on the other side of town, and as an aid to the exclusion of Sid, who refused to be mute or invisible, I began to remember how it used to be with Beth and me in the pre-Thatcher days, and there wasn't really anything remarkable about it or us or anything we did, but it seemed remarkable at the time, and still did at times like now, and this is the way, to put it clearly, it was.

Beth had been a girl around town, born there and growing up there, and I had known her since way back. She had always been the kind of girl that boys notice, even back in elementary school days when she was a very small girl being noticed by very small boys, but later, sometime in high school, she was suddenly the loveliest girl in the world. This was an opinion I shared with many others, and the truth of the opinion was something we felt instinctively and passionately, although we had never seen all the other girls in the world, or even a fair share of them. She had this pale hair and these brown eyes that seemed sometimes in the light to be almost golden, and she had a natural way of walking that some women have to learn at great expense as an essential element of their professional equipment. It is a way that is difficult and almost impossible to describe, but you have seen it in the best actresses and models, and it has in it a kind of complete grace and vibrancy that communicates itself without excessive intrusion of moving parts.

I was lucky then, in high school, for Beth took a fancy to me that was somewhat greater than, if not exclusive of, the fancies she had in varying degrees for others. Well, you can't ask for everything. If I didn't get all of what then passed for love, I at least got more than my share, and it was in this early period of ancient history, along toward the end of it, that we stopped now and again, while passing through Dreamer's Park, for the modest frolics in the old bandstand which I had mentioned in telecon, and to which I was now headed by shank's mare.

Soon after that we entered the middle period of this ancient era, and this period lasted for nine years and was characterized mainly by my absence from town. I spent most of seven of the nine at the state university in pre-law and law, which made me twenty-five, and then I worked two more for the Adjutant-General, which made me twenty-seven. I was released, as they say, under honorable conditions, and came home. End of middle period.

I had seen Beth now and then during this time, of course, but not often and never for long, and in the final eighteen months of it, not at all. Now I was home to stay, honorable but undistinguished, never even having met the Adjutant-General, and there was Beth still. If she was not exactly waiting for me, still she was there. She was more or less engaged, in fact, to Sherman Pike, who was about my age and who had become editor of the

Record, the local daily, during my absence. Sherm had a good brain and considerable talent, a fine and sensitive fellow, and it was generally conceded that he had a fair prospect of becoming important. I admit that I had been anticipating more of Beth, having learned, as I aged, a lot more about the interesting things you can do with women, even to marrying them, but I was prepared, after I discovered how matters had developed with her and Sherm, to concede and withdraw all claims and look elsewhere for diversion.

But Beth wouldn't have it that way. Her fancy for Gideon Jones was still strong, although not exclusive, and pretty soon we had taken up what we had never quite put down, and it was better than ever and kept getting better than that. It didn't last long, not quite a year, which was the time of the third and final pre-Thatcher period, but it was hot while it lasted, and I began to think about marriage just as soon as my infant practice became able to toddle, and we even tried a few samples that we both liked fine.

It was too bad about Sherm, but as things turned out, it didn't make much difference to him, anyhow, for it wasn't more than four or five months after my return when he went home one evening and died. He had had rheumatic fever as a boy, and the doctor said that it was an impaired heart that caused it. He was buried on a Wednesday afternoon, having had no time to become important after all, in the cemetery on the east edge of town. I went and Beth went, but we didn't go together.

I had no reason to think that things would be different between us, and they weren't. Not, that is, until the very end of that brief and final period.

Everything was satisfactory, even intense and exciting. Beth went out a couple of times with Wilson Thatcher, and I raised a mild sort of hell about it, but she said it was only for a little variety and to help him spend a little money, of which I was short constantly and he never. Then, to get it over with, there was the night when they got married, and that was the end of it. For seven years at least.

I won't go into those seven years, except to say that they were rather distressing in the beginning, and I wished that it had been I who died of an impaired heart instead of Sherman Pike. My own was impaired, I felt, but I didn't die of it, and when Sid came along I was glad I hadn't. We were married after a while, and it was a good marriage, and I thought of Beth only now and then.

Until tonight, that is, when I tried to think of her exclusively in the evasion of my conscience. This sad summer night of gin and cicadas at the end of seven years. Walking through the night across the town in spite of common sense and Sid.

5

In your own town, if it is a town of a certain size and character, you probably have a Dreamer's Park. It is not a large park, occupying only a square block, and it is thickly planted with indigenous trees, possibly oaks and maples and elms and sycamores. Gravel paths, bordered with red bricks set edgewise in the earth, cross the park diagonally from corner to corner, and various gravel tributaries branch off less geometrically from these. Wooden benches with cast-iron legs and arms, the seats and backs constructed of heavy slats, are scattered over the grass beneath the trees, and in one corner, where two streets join, there are a couple of clay tennis courts that are usually not in very good condition. The grass is cut once in a while, but it never has the neat, clipped appearance of golf courses and modern cemeteries. In the center of the park, so that the two diagonal paths must coincide briefly to make their ways around it in a circle, is a wooden bandstand needing paint and repair.

The park is old, as age is reckoned in your town, and not so much use is made of it now as used to be. A few children play there on warm, dry days. A few families or other groups have picnics under the trees on summer evenings. The tennis courts are used occasionally by poor players who are not particular, but there are better courts for better players other places. The green benches under the trees are mostly occupied by old men who have nothing much to do, and who walk there slowly to sit and rest and doze and dream before walking slowly home again. At night, sometimes, lovers stop by.

There are no concerts in the bandstand nowadays, but once, a number of years ago, there was one every Friday night of the warm months from May to September. The concert was played by the town band under the direction of the high school music teacher, who was paid extra for this extra service, and he was glad to have the job because he needed the money. People came from all over town to hear the concerts, sitting on the benches and the grass and in parked cars along the four bounding streets, and quite a thing was made of them. The program was printed in the newspaper Thursday evening, so that everyone might know exactly what he could expect to hear, and temporary refreshment stands were erected for the sale of ice cream cones and candy bars and soda pop.

The kids ran around the park and sometimes became noisy enough to interfere with the listening pleasure of their elders, but this was not a serious problem and was generally tolerated with reasonably good grace. The program varied somewhat from week to week, but there were several favorites that reappeared regularly, and almost every concert ended with a stirring rendition, heavy on trumpets and trombones, of Sousa's 'Stars and Stripes Forever.' Once each season, near Memorial Day, there was a tenor in the band who laid aside his instrument long enough to sing 'My Buddy.'

Nights are long since you went away,
I dream about you all through the
    day,
My buddy,
My buddy,
Your buddy misses you.

Something like that. The tenor was usually not very true, and the amplifiers didn't help any in that respect, but the song was appreciated especially by the veterans, which may even have included then, if you are old enough now, someone from Shiloh or Antietam or Gettysburg.

This was Dreamer's Park, to which I was going, and after a while I got there. I entered the park at its south east corner, reaching the diagonal gravel walk, and it was dark in there under the trees on the walk leading to the heart of the darkness. My heels made crunching sounds on the gravel, and I kept listening for other sounds around me, breathing or whispering or the breathless laughing of lovers, but I couldn't hear a thing, or see a thing except the trunks of trees and the deeper shadow of the bandstand ahead of me, and then after a few seconds I became aware of a soft and sibilant sound, a kind of hissing, and it was me whistling through my teeth for company.

Arriving at the bandstand, I went a quarter of a turn around the circle and up rickety steps. The stand was also circular, with a shingled peaked roof, and all around the perimeter was a built-in bench that was no more than a hard seat braced at intervals from the floor with two-by-fours, open space between the seat and the floor. I sat down on the bench and began to wait, looking out into the park and listening for the sound of Beth's feet on the gravel walk, but the only sounds I heard came from the four streets beyond, where cars and pedestrians passed sparsely in four directions.

I wondered why Beth was so late, for the hotel from which she would come was much nearer than my house in Hoolihan's Addition, but then I realized that she had probably delayed deliberately in order to avoid doing what I was doing instead, which was waiting alone in this dark park. It was pretty creepy there, as a matter of fact, and I wanted to light a cigarette but decided that maybe I better hadn't, and then, having decided against it, I was immediately beset by the strongest longing to smoke imaginable, although I am an undedicated smoker who can ordinarily take or leave a cigarette without the slightest trauma.

Time passed. So, on the four streets, did the sparse cars, the sparse pedestrians. And so, in the bandstand, did the expectations of Gideon Jones, who had been tricked and traduced in the tradition of the past into recurrent jackassery. Not, I believed sincerely, that Beth had done this, then or now, in deliberate malice or cruelty or even indifference.

She had merely submitted on impulse to circumstances that had arisen without her contriving. She had merely met someone else and gone another place, just as she had once met and married another man and gone to California. It was all done with a kind of pathological innocence in the most amiable way.

I stood up and walked across the bandstand to the other side, my steps a truncated series of hollow sounds on rotting boards. The last step brought the toe of my right foot into the space beneath the circular bench, and it made contact suddenly with something soft but substantial down there on the floor. I stood for a moment with breath and motion suspended, and then I breathed and backed away a step and bent down. There was something down there, all right, under the bench, and I touched reluctantly what felt like flesh. Soft flesh beneath my fingertips.

Nose, eyes, mouth. Sinking down all the way onto my knees, I struck a match and looked at Beth beneath the bench, Beth's face with open, empty eyes, and somehow I was not in the least surprised. The match burned my fingers, and I let it fall.

What did I think? Well, I thought that it was just like Beth, by God, to come to such a sticky end, and that she had surely come in amiable innocence to die with utter wonder that anyone on earth would wish her dead. I thought that it was too bad to kill her, and that whoever had done it should be ashamed of himself. I thought that now I would never have the chance to say goodbye to her properly, never in this world. I thought that I had better get the hell away from there if I knew what was good for me.

I stood and turned and went, leaving her lying where she was, a long way in the end from Miami and Rio and Acapulco and places like that. I walked directly home, the precise route in reverse that I had come, and the cicadas were silent in the trees, and the sad summer night was sour.

The house was dark, which signified that Sid was still involved with Rose Pogue and Zoroaster, unless she had returned and gone to bed already, which was unlikely. Going to bed was something I had in mind for myself, although it would be impossible to sleep, for I wanted to be there when Sid got back in order to practice the simple deception of being what I was not, an innocent husband at rest, and I might, by keeping my eyes closed and my breathing deep, avoid the ordeal of casual conversation or the now impossible demands of an interesting time.

I went upstairs and undressed in the dark and got into my side of the bed and lay there under a sheet thinking. My thinking, however, was not very clear or coherent, and the truth is that I didn't know what to do, or if I had been smart or stupid in doing what I had already done. I knew that I should have reported Beth's death to the police, of course, but anyone can see that this would have involved tricky explanations that I preferred to avoid if possible. I felt guilty about going off and leaving her alone on the hard floor of the bandstand in the darkness of Dreamer's Park, and there was a thin little voice in my brain that kept saying I could at least have seen to it that she was taken somewhere and made comfortable for the night, but this was sentiment unrelated to circumstances or sense. It could hardly be expected that Beth would ever know or care that I had or hadn't, and besides, considered from a particular point of view, it was a kind of dirty trick she had pulled on me, anyhow.

And not the first, either, although the last.

What I was in, plainly, was a mess. Someone had killed her, and I had walked into it full of gin and nostalgia with nothing more on my mind than a minor infidelity, and who had done it, for whatever reason, was something that might never be known if I became involved and placed at the scene, for it might be decided that I was as logical as anyone else could be, besides being convenient. If this developed, as it might, it would certainly be advisable to have some alternate suggestions in mind, and I tried to think of some alternates to suggest, but the best I could do on short notice was Wilson Thatcher, who wasn't very convincing in the part.

More likely, I thought, it was someone with a good reason who had followed Beth here from wherever she had been, or most likely of all, it was a local glandular nut who had followed her to the park or had simply discovered her there by accident in the dark bandstand. Still, as I remembered her in the brief and tiny flare of the match, she had shown no signs of struggle or abuse. No bruises or abrasions or torn clothing. Neither had her face in its final expression shown any of the agony or distortions that are supposed to be left by strangulation, which would have been a reasonable technique in a murder that no one had particularly anticipated or planned. There had been only the expression of wonder that this was actually happening to Beth Webb Thatcher, who had lately been living well in various pleasant places.

It occurred to me then that I had no acceptable evidence, aside from her being dead, that she had been killed at all. And being dead is really no evidence of having been killed, for it is possible to be dead from merely having died.

Remembering as clearly as I could as many details as I had seen, I could recall no blood, no wound, not even any bumps. Was it possible that Beth had simply and suddenly died? Some kind of attack or something?

This theory, unlikely as it might seem, had a convincing quality as applied to Beth, for it was exactly the kind of innocent imposition I wouldn't have put past her. Nevertheless, I rejected the theory. The odds against it, I thought, were far too great to discount for even so unpredictable a long-shot as she. She had been lying on her back, under the bench where she must have been pushed, and somewhere on her backside, where I couldn't see it, there was surely the mark of whatever had killed her.

I wished Sid would come home. I was in no mood for conversation or entertainment, but I was more than ready to welcome a warm and sympathetic presence. Just someone around. Someone I could watch covertly, pretending sleep, as she went about the delightful business of preparing herself for her half of the bed. Someone to lie lightly and breathe softly and sleep sweetly beside me. Not just someone, either. Sid or no one.

Specifically Sid, and here she came.

I heard the car in the drive and the steps on the stairs, and I was thinking realistically when she came into the room that she would surely be neither warm nor sympathetic if the events of the night became known. After lighting a small lamp on her dressing table, she stood with her hands on her hips looking at me. I had turned my head to a position to see her, and I could see her fuzzily through slits and lashes.

'Well, I'll be damned,' she said.

She walked over to the bed and bent over and examined me thoroughly. She bent nearer and sniffed.

'Stoned,' she said. 'After giving me every reason to expect something special, he's drunk himself into an absolute stupor in which nothing can be expected of him at all.'

She went away into the bathroom, and I could hear water running in there, and a brisk, bristly little sound that was caused, I guessed, by the brushing of her teeth. Pretty soon she came back barefooted, having kicked off her white flats, and got out of what she was in, and into what passed for a nightgown. In the gown, a blue shortie with tiny white rosebuds here and there, she returned to the bed and sat down on the edge and again examined me critically.

'It's simply an intolerable disappointment,' she said, 'and I've a good mind to waken him.'

She considered this for a minute, whether to waken me or not, and then she decided that she would. She shook me by the shoulder pretty hard, but I kept my eyes closed in simulation of the stupor she had charged me with, and after several seconds she stopped shaking. I kept on lying there with my eyes closed, thinking that I had convinced her, but then there was a small and painful explosion on my left cheek which was repeated instantly on my right cheek, and I knew that she had merely stepped up her attack, God only knowing what she would resort to next if necessary. It seemed to me that simulation had become entirely too risky to sustain, and so I groaned and opened my eyes and groaned again.

'What the hell's the matter with you, sugar?' she said. 'Why have you gone to bed and to sleep in spite of all our plans?'

'I'm sick,' I said.

She laced her hands around a knee and

71

rocked back on her pretty pivot with a derisive expression.

'Sick? You're loaded, sugar. That's what you are.'

'Nothing of the sort. I had a few more gimlets, I admit, but I'm not loaded.'

'Where are you sick?'

'It's my stomach. Something terrific is going on down there.'

'Well, you can hardly expect to drink gimlet after gimlet for hour after hour without having something go on in your stomach. What you need is a big dose of Kaopectate.'

'Like hell I do.'

'Sugar, you mustn't be cowardly about it. When you deliberately get your stomach in an uproar, you must be prepared to take something for it afterward. A dose of Kaopectate is good for anyone at times.'

'Not for me. I don't want any God damn Kaopectate, and I refuse to have any.'

'Nonsense. You'll take a big dose immediately, and later you'll be glad.'

She got up and went into the bathroom

again and rattled around and came back with a bottle and a spoon.

'Where in the devil did you get the spoon?' I said. 'Have you moved the kitchen upstairs?'

'Of course not. That's ridiculous. I always keep a spoon in the medicine cabinet for emergencies. When you have a husband who swills gin by the gallon, you never know when it will be needed.'

'Well, I know when it will *not* be needed, and now is when. Take that stuff away from here.'

'Don't be difficult, sugar. There's no need to be contentious because your belly hurts.'

'I'm being contentious because I'm determined not to take any Kaopectate.'

'That's absurd. Sit up, now, and open your mouth. Don't make me spill it.'

She poured a spoonful of the stuff and poked it at me. In order to avoid getting soaked, I sat up and opened my mouth and permitted her to pour it down my throat. The taste of Kaopectate is really not so bad as tastes go, but I was excessively offended by it this time because it was unnecessary, my claim to a sick stomach being a plain lie.

'There you are,' she said. 'That wasn't so bad, was it?'

'Bad enough.'

'You'll be feeling much better shortly. Wait and see.'

'There being nothing else I can do, I will.'

She went away with the bottle and spoon and came back without them. Sitting down on the edge of the bed in the same place and position, she watched me for a while without speaking, and I began to feel uncomfortable.

'Are you feeling any better yet?' she said.

'Not yet.'

'It's too bad of you to make such a pig of yourself. It's evident that nothing of interest can be expected of you tonight. You've spoiled everything.'

'I might point out that matters would have been different if you had been willing to give up Rose Pogue and Zoroaster.'

'I suppose I must treat you like a baby

and be with you every minute. It does seem, however, that you should be able to behave yourself without being under constant surveillance. The wonder is, I suppose, that you weren't into more mischief than you were.'

'It would be impossible for me to be in more mischief than I was, and the mischief I was in was mischief enough, believe me.'

'What do you mean? I don't like the sound of it. What did you do besides drink and drink and get your belly in an uproar? What else?'

I had not intended to go off in this direction, and I was simply gone before I knew it. I scrapped deception without considering the consequences, and I think the reason I did it was because I had to have a confidant even at the risk of losing a wife. I admit freely that I just wasn't made for the solitary bearing of bad trouble and grim possibilities.

'What else I did,' I said, 'was meet Beth Thatcher in the old bandstand in Dreamer's Park. At least I went there to meet her, although I didn't, as it turned out. I had been drinking gimlets and listening to 'Death and Transfiguration,' and then the phone rang, and I answered it, and it was Beth. She said she was leaving tomorrow and wanted to see me tonight to say a proper goodbye, and a lot of things were working together to make me go. She was the one who suggested Dreamer's Park, and I went there to meet her, but I didn't because she was dead.'

I was still sitting up against the headboard in the position I had assumed for taking Kaopectate, and she was still sitting on the edge of the bed in her blue shortie with white rosebuds, and we sat there looking at each other after my confession, and I was pretty sure that I wasn't going to get absolution at the moment, if ever. She didn't appear to be exceptionally angry, hardly at all, but I wasn't fooled by this, having known her pretty well for some time, and she was probably thinking, in spite of her deceptive, serene gravity, what a pleasure it would be to attend my funeral after having personally got me ready for it.

'As for me,' she said at last, 'I am not so

concerned with your having found her dead as I am with what you would have done if you hadn't.'

'There's no use speculating about that, so far as I can see. She was dead, and nothing was done.'

'On the contrary, there's a great deal of use in speculating about it. One could very easily reach some interesting conclusions, although the range of possibilities of what could be done in a dark park is so broad that it almost staggers the imagination. One thing seems certain to begin with. It would scarcely have been necessary to meet there to say a proper goodbye. It would be, in my judgment, far more appropriate to an *im*proper goodbye.'

'Oh, come off, Sid. Beth's dead, and I'm in trouble, and all you can think about is some damn peccadillo that didn't even happen.'

'You're in trouble, all right, sugar. You're perfectly right there. Unless, that is, you can explain satisfactorily why it was necessary to say goodbye in a dark park instead of some place like a hotel lobby or a lighted street corner or the reading room of the YWCA.'

'Damn it, there was nothing of any consequence intended. You know how this town is, and what would have been said about us if we had been seen together even in a crowded tabernacle. We merely wanted to avoid gossip, that's all, and Dreamer's Park was just a place that occurred to her and seemed reasonable to me because it's a place we had been before, a long time ago, and a place where couples still go now and then.'

'I know that couples go there, and I know what for. Not, as a regular thing, to say a proper goodbye. Your explanation, however, is just ridiculous enough to seem characteristic, and I'll consider accepting it. But now, I suppose, I had better consider the rest of the matter. You've made a mess of things by drinking gin and sneaking off in the night to meet someone who turned up dead, and it's plain that I must consider what's to be done about it. Isn't it expected of a person who finds a body to report it to the police or someone?'

'Yes, it is. It's expected.'

'Then why, may I ask, didn't you do what was expected?'

'Because she was dead from having been killed. Because I wanted to avoid offering myself up to suspicion of having killed her. It would probably be difficult to explain to a cop how I just happened to be in that damn park at such an hour.'

'That's true. It's even difficult to explain it to me.'

'Oh, well, I've told you the truth. I couldn't tell it to anyone else without stirring up a lot of wrong ideas.'

'I'm not so sure your confidence in me is justified, sugar. You have certainly stirred up a lot of ideas, at any rate, wrong or not. Wouldn't it have shown you were innocent if you reported finding the body?'

'Not necessarily. They'd be sure to think it might be a trick.'

'I doubt that you'd be seriously considered a suspect, sugar. A man who is too cowardly to take a dose of Kaopectate would hardly commit a murder.'

'That may be true, but the police are

not aware of the intimate details of my relationship with Kaopectate.'

'How was she killed, by the way?'

'I don't know. I only saw her for a few seconds by the light of a match, and I didn't see any wound or anything.'

'Then how the hell do you know she was killed at all?'

'I've thought about it, and it seems probable.'

'I agree that it does. Dreamer's Park in the middle of the night is hardly a place where one would go deliberately to die naturally. Do you know what I think?'

'No. What?'

'I think that there is nothing to be done except let things work out as they will. Perhaps everything will be settled without any great unpleasantness to anyone except the murderer, if they catch him, and if bad comes to worse, you are at least a lawyer and can defend yourself competently.'

'Thanks. That's very reassuring.'

'How are you feeling now?'

'Cheerful and confident. I always feel cheerful and confident after finding a body under incriminating circumstances.'

'I mean your stomach, sugar.'

'Oh. My stomach's all right. It's fine.'

'You see? Kaopectate works wonders.'

She went over and turned off the little light on her dressing table and came back and lay down beside me in the darkness. I could hear her breathing evenly, and smell the light sweet scent of her, and after a while feel the soft warmth of her, and we lay there for a while quietly before she spoke again.

'Sugar,' she said, 'is it possible that you killed her after all?'

'One could conceivably believe it.'

'A few minutes ago you said that one couldn't.'

'I know, but I've been thinking it over, and I've decided that it's possible. After all, I am as unlikely a murderer as you, and if she were here alive at this moment, I'm sure I would kill her with pleasure.'

6

I woke early after going to sleep late. Sid was still asleep on her side, curled like a cold child in a sprinkling of white rosebuds, and I got out of bed quietly and stood for a minute watching her, and I was sorry for what had happened, and I wished that it hadn't, but it had. There was a bad taste in my mouth, and an ache between my eyes. Outside, in the bright light of morning, a cardinal was screeching his pointed red head off, and I remembered a book about birds that I used to have when I was a kid that said the call of the cardinal was telling everyone to cheer up, cheer up, and I thought to myself now, listening to this one, *Like hell I will.*

I went into the bathroom and bathed and shaved and brushed, and then I returned to the bedroom and dressed, and all the while Sid kept on sleeping on her side. It seemed to me that she was a little too perfectly the picture of sleeping, her body so still and her breath so measured, and I wondered if she was only pretending, as I had tried to do last night, until I was gone the hell away. I didn't have the heart to blame her if she was, and if there had been any feasible and physical way to accomplish it, I'd have gone the hell away from myself.

Since there was none, I decided that I would at least find myself a little more tolerable if I were full of hot coffee, and so I went downstairs to the kitchen and put on the pot.

I drank the coffee black, two cups, after which I went out into the hall to the foot of the stairs and stood listening for some sound of life above, but there wasn't any. There didn't seem to be anything left to do but go, and so I went, walking, and it was still pretty early when I reached my office.

It was a substantial hour before Millie was scheduled to report, and it would probably be longer than that this morning because of the engineer last night. This meant that I would have a considerable while to spend with myself, who had come with me in spite of not being wanted, and I spent it watching the Rexall sign across the street and wondering when Beth would be found, if she hadn't been found already, and who would find her if someone else hadn't. An hour and a half had passed when Millie came, half an hour late, and it took her ten minutes more to get from her desk to mine. She looked fairly fresh and alert, and smug enough to justify the assumption that something pleasant had recently happened to her.

'Good morning, Mr. Jones,' she said.

'Is it?' I said. 'Or is it afternoon?'

'Oh, oh.' She cocked her red head and looked at me warily. 'You've got bags under your eyes.'

'So have you.'

'I was up all hours. Were you?'

'Never mind. How was the engineer?'

'Determined. Original, too. He was interesting and challenging but not entirely successful. I think he'll be back to try again.'

'Next time, give in. That way you'll get

to bed earlier and to work on time.'

'Well, aren't we sour this morning! What the hell happened to you last night?'

'Nothing.'

'Nothing? Then that explains everything. That's the worst kind of night of all.'

In my opinion, she was wrong, and I could have cited instances of recent happenings to support my opinion, but I didn't feel like continuing the discussion.

Having had the last word, to which she was welcome, she went back to her desk in the outer office, and a few minutes later I could hear the busy sound of her typewriter. The morning got going, much as other mornings had been getting going for something like seven years, and by ten-fifteen, at which time Millie took a break for coffee in the Hotel Carson coffee shop, I had consulted an elderly citizen about the terms of his will, conducted a long telephone conversation with an insurance investigator about the conditions of an accident in which a client of mine was involved, and had undertaken to get a waiver on the three-day waiting period for a young couple who had a good reason for wanting to get married in a hurry.

When Millie returned at ten-forty, ten minutes late, I was doing some desk work on the defense of a local tavern owner who had been caught in his back room with his dice showing. It wasn't much of a case, and there wasn't much of a defense, except that the tavern owner was good to his mother, and this appeal was somewhat compromised by the fact that mother herself had been shooting craps in the back room when the cops moved in.

Millie came on directly into my office, and I could see at once by her glittering eyes that she had been stimulated during her absence by a hell of a lot more than caffeine.

'The most shocking thing has happened,' she said. 'I heard all about it in the coffee shop.'

'Shocking things are happening all the time everywhere,' I said. 'Fighting in Africa. Fighting in Laos. Firing squads in Cuba. Men in orbit here and there. The whole God damn world in orbit. To what particularly shocking thing that you learned all about in the coffee shop are you referring?'

'Oh, well, I keep forgetting that you're an important educated lawyer and are not interested in anything less than a world event.' She hooked half of her bottom on the edge of my desk and inspected the fingernails of her right hand. 'This is only local, of course, but it might turn into some work for you. A fat fee, I mean. Judging from last month's receipts, you could probably use it.'

'I'm intrigued. What local event that might turn into work?'

'You remember Beth Webb Thatcher? I think you used to know her.'

'You know damn well I used to know her. I used to go with her fairly regularly. In fact, exclusively. I used to think for a while that I was going to marry her, but I didn't, and I'm glad. This is all ancient history.'

'Well, now she's dead. This is modern history. In fact, as the saying goes, it's current events. This morning a couple of kids went into Dreamer's Park to play, and after a while they got around to playing in the old band stand, and there she was. Beth. Dead. They ran home and told their parents, who called the cops, who went out there and discovered that someone had slipped a long, thin blade into her from behind, and she had died of it. Just imagine. All this was happening while an engineer was happening to me and nothing at all was happening to you.'

I thought I was prepared for it, but it made me sick. I guess I showed it, pallor or something, for Millie unhooked her bottom from the desk and came around and hooked it on the arm of my chair and put an arm around my shoulders. She made little repentant noises in her throat.

'I'm sorry, Gid,' she said. 'I'm just a bitch, that's what I am. I hope I get cancer of the tongue from smoking unfiltered cigarettes.'

'Think nothing of it,' I said. 'It's no more than the natural shock of learning that someone you once went with exclusively with the intention of marrying has died suddenly from having a long, thin blade slipped into her from behind.'

'You're a good boss and an understanding fellow,' she said, 'and I love you.'

'I'm all in favor of that,' I said. 'If there's anything I need at the moment it's love.'

'Shall I lock the door?' she said.

'Well, no,' I said. 'It's platonic love I need.'

I went on sitting there, pale or something, and she went on sitting there beside me, hooked on the arm, with her arm around me. I was grateful for the arm, grateful for her bright red head and all the rest of her, and even grateful for Plato, who gave it a name and kept it decent.

'Who do you suppose did it?' she said.

'I don't know. Local legend gives me a kind of reason, but I'm innocent. That's all I know on short notice.'

'It may have been a nut of some kind. That's always possible and frequently convenient.'

'I thought of that first thing.'

'What?'

'First thing after you told me.'

'That's fast thinking, boss. It shows that reason can rise above emotion. If someone comes to trial for it, maybe you can get the case, and I can get a raise. A thing like this could make you famous. Another Clarence Darrow or somebody like that.'

'Sure. Think of all the human interest.'

'That's what I mean. Young lawyer defends man charged with murder of old sweetie. Young lawyer's sweetie, I mean. That will need revision, however. A young lawyer wouldn't have an old sweetie, would he? A young lawyer would surely have a young sweetie.'

'This young lawyer doesn't have any sweetie at all. This young lawyer has a wife.'

'So you do. And a damn nice one, too. I admit this reluctantly.'

'What else did you hear in the coffee shop?'

'Not much. Only that Beth came to town yesterday. Only that everyone is wondering why, and no one seems to know.'

'Also that everyone, by this time, knows

that she and I had two gimlets together in the Kiowa Room yesterday evening.'

'Gimlets? Two of them? It's good to know the facts. I've heard everything from Martinis to Daiquiris and from one to six.'

'That's interesting. Did you hear anyone say that I killed her?'

'Not exactly. All I heard was one man say that you *should* have killed her if you didn't. He was a friend.'

'Some friend,' I said bitterly.

At that moment, someone came into the outer office, and Millie went out to see who it was. I waited for her to come back and tell me, but she didn't. Sid came instead.

'Sugar,' she said, 'I've come down to have lunch with you.'

'You're welcome,' I said, 'but it's too early for lunch.'

She came around my desk and kissed me with sufficient warmth to make me feel wanted again, and I held her for a minute, smelling her hair. We were standing for this, and pretty soon I sat down in my chair with her in my lap, and

I continued to hold her with one arm. She was wearing several shades of brown from light to dark in various places from hat to shoes, all of which went well with a tan suit for summer. The narrow skirt of the tan suit rode up a little above her tan nylon knees, and I put my free hand on the nearer knee.

'I've been feeling perfectly miserable,' she said.

'Have you? So have I, and for a good reason. What's yours?'

'Do you remember when you got up this morning?'

'I remember. I had a bad taste in my mouth and a bad ache between my eyes, and there was a loud-mouthed cardinal outside the window.'

'Sugar, I'm sorry. How is the ache between your eyes now?'

'Gone.'

'I'm so glad. Did you take an aspirin or anything?'

'No. Just two cups of black coffee.'

'Coffee is good, all right. If I had been a sensible wife, I'd have gotten up and made it for you.'

'Oh, nonsense. You were sleeping beautifully, on your side like a child, and so I left you alone.'

'No. That's not true, and it's what I've been feeling miserable about. The truth is, I wasn't asleep at all. I was only pretending.'

'I thought you might be, but I wasn't sure. You lay so still and breathed so quietly. Normally a person jerks and snorts a little over a period of time while sleeping.'

'Do I jerk and snort? Honestly?'

'A little. Delicately, however. Nothing crude.'

'I'm glad of that, at least. If I must jerk and snort in my sleep, I'm at least glad I do it delicately. Anyhow, I was deceptive and cowardly to pretend sleeping, and you were no sooner gone than I wished I hadn't done it.'

'That's all right. I don't blame you for wanting to avoid me. I would have avoided myself if it had been possible.'

'You shouldn't be *too* self-critical, sugar. It makes a bad impression. What you must do is concentrate on your good qualities. You have a number that I can name if you wish.'

'Thanks very much, but I think it will be more therapeutic if I can discover them for myself.'

'In the meanwhile, will you answer honestly a candid question?'

'All right. I'll answer honestly.'

'If Beth had been alive when you went to meet her last night, what would you have done? That's the question.'

'Well, it's a tough question, honey, but here's my honest answer. We'd have talked, and maybe held hands and kissed and got sloppy about the past, and then we'd have said goodbye, and she'd have gone away, and I'd have been glad that she was gone. That's the truth as I am now truly convinced.'

'Sugar, you have said exactly the right thing. I believe you, and the whole episode, so far as I'm concerned, is no more than an example of the peculiar kind of idiocy that is natural to men at times. I even feel rather tender toward you for being such a chump. What we have to concentrate on now, since this has been settled satisfactorily, is how to keep you out of trouble if possible, or how to *get* you out of trouble if it becomes necessary.'

'I've been thinking myself that this problem should have priority.'

'Good. We're agreed on that, then, and we're again, I hope, on the best of terms.'

'Well, God damn it, I'm madly in love with you, non-platonic style. You may call that being on the best of terms if you choose.'

'I do, sugar. There are absolutely no terms better. And now I'm determined on going to lunch, early or not. I had no breakfast at all, I was feeling so miserable, but now I'm feeling much better and too hungry to wait. What time is it? Couldn't you leave now?'

'It's eleven, and I could.'

'Let's go, then. We'll have a drink before lunch, that's what we'll do. Not gimlets, however. Not even gin. We'll have a Daiquiri or a sidecar or something.'

She stood up and tugged at her stockings and smoothed her skirt over her hips, after which, while I put away some papers, she repaired her lips with a lipstick that she took from her purse, peering for the purpose into the tiny mirror of a compact, also from the purse. Then we went into the outer office, and I told Millie where I was going in general, out to lunch, and if I wasn't back by twelve to lock the door and go out to lunch herself. This wasn't really necessary, for she would have gone anyhow when her time came, but such gestures of consideration helped sustain an amiable atmosphere around the office. She said all right, and Sid and I went on downstairs to the street, which was hot and full of sunshine.

'Where do you want to go?' I said.

'The hotel, I guess. Is there someplace else near?'

'There are other places, but I don't recommend them. At the hotel, however, we have a choice of the coffee shop or the Kiowa Room.'

'The Kiowa Room for lunch? It's a bar, sugar, as you know far better than most.'

'I know, but they've begun setting up a buffet in there for lunch. You can get stuffed for a dollar.'

'Really? I didn't know that.'

'It's a kind of special attraction for businessmen and such. Do you want to try it?'

'Yes, I do. There's nothing that appeals to me more than submitting to temptation, and I can't think of anything more calculated than a buffet to make me submit.'

'Thanks, honey. There's nothing like running second to beef stroganoff.'

'You shouldn't take it personally, sugar. I meant at lunchtime only. You are excluded in any event, but you'll have to admit that we're a little past the nooner period.'

I wasn't so sure of that, but anyhow this wasn't one of the noons, and so we went on over to the hotel and into the Kiowa Room. The buffet was laid out, and the tables were covered with white cloths, places already set, and there were a few people already eating, but not many because it was still early.

Sid and I served ourselves and found a table in a corner, and a girl who came to pour coffee was induced to run an errand to the bar. She came back with a couple of sidecars, which were what Sid decided we should have, and we emptied our glasses slowly and started on our plates. We hadn't said anything since entering the room, not a word to each other, but our silence was warm and comfortable, and everything was fine for the present, even though later it might not be.

People kept passing with full plates on the way to somewhere to sit.

'Do you know what I would like to do this afternoon?' Sid finally said.

'No,' I said. 'What?'

'I'd like to go swimming and lie in the sun.'

'I wish I could go, but I can't.'

'Couldn't you possibly arrange it? I have a strong urging to go.'

'I can't possibly. There's some work I have to finish on a case I'm sure to lose, and at three o'clock I have an appointment with a man who wants to sue another man. But you go on, anyhow. I'll think about you and wish I were there.'

'No. I don't want to go without you. I

won't go, and that's all there is to it. I'll go home and sit in the sun on the back terrace, and afterward I'll have a cold shower. That's always pleasant, and besides, while I'm sitting in the sun I can go over my notes on Zoroaster. They're rather confusing right now, and need to be straightened out in my mind.

'Do you know how Zoroaster was born? His guardian angel somehow got into a priest, and there was a heavenly ray of some sort that got into a beautiful noble girl at the same time. Later on, this priest and this girl got together and made love, and the guardian angel in the priest and the heavenly ray in the girl got mixed together, and Zoroaster was the result. Do you think it could have happened that way?'

'Who knows? Perhaps you aren't supposed to take it literally.'

'That may be. Anyhow, what's worrying me is how to put it so some member of the discussion group won't be offended. It's a little sexy when you come right down to it. Do you have any suggestions?'

'I don't think anyone will be offended if

you use plenty of euphemisms.'

'Euphemism? Isn't that a word that means the same as a word that sounds worse?'

'That's it.'

'I suppose that could be done, all right. I'll think about it while sitting in the sun. Fortunately, the way he was born is the only sticky part. There's no problem involved in the way he died. It's very simple and dramatic, although incredible, which will make no difference to Christians who are not prepared to believe it, anyhow. Do you know how he died? He lived to be very old, and then he was struck by lightning and ascended into heaven.'

'I remember a little about it. The Persians called him Zarathustra, I think, and so did Nietzsche.'

'What does Nietzsche have to do with it? Who was he? I don't recall that Rose and I came across him anywhere in what we read.'

'Nietzsche was a German philosopher. He doesn't have anything to do with it directly. He just used the name in the title of a book a long time later.'

'Well, it just shows you how ignorant I am. I'm surprised that Rose didn't mention him, however. She's very intellectual, as you know, and she usually mentions everything and everyone that can be connected with anything or anyone.'

'Rose is a schoolteacher, and it's expected of her to be intellectual.'

'She only teaches second grade. Is it expected of teachers who teach second grade to know about Zoroaster?'

'Possibly not. I admit that Rose is an exceptional second grade teacher . . . Sugar, are you sure you can't take the afternoon off?'

'Not completely off. But maybe I can get through early.'

'That's something, at least. I'll tell you what I'll do. I'll pick you up in the car, and we'll drive straight home. Will you be finished by four with the man who wants to sue another man?'

'Finished and waiting.'

Oh, well. That's the way it went, and there's no point in going on with it. We ate lunch and said things and made dry love. It was wonderful because it was wonderful. We never mentioned what was in the back of our minds, sometimes in the front, and I knew that she had come downtown to meet me and have lunch with me in a public place because she knew that what had happened would dredge up old matters, unpleasant at best and disastrous at worst, and she was making in her own way in this public place a public declaration that it was going to be, to poach on Dumas, one for two and two for one.

I was profoundly grateful for what she was doing and what she was, for what she was doing was wonderful, as I said, and what she was, was little and lovely and tough as a boot.

7

As it turned out, the three-o'clock appointment was canceled, which was a relief, and I decided about that time that I'd call Sid and have her come on down and pick me up. I had my telephone out of its cradle and my index finger pointed at the dial when Millie cracked the door to the outer office and poked her red head through the crack.

'There's a man here to see you,' she said.

'I don't want to see a man. I want to go home, and that's where I'm going.'

'Well, I've got a notion this may not be a simple matter of what you want or don't want. I've got a notion it's going to be sort of compulsory.'

'Why the hell don't you try being reasonably direct and lucid for a change? State his name and business.'

'His name is Cotton McBride, and his business is being a policeman. Not just an ordinary policeman, either. He's no less than a detective.'

'Damn it, I know who and what Cotton McBride is. Did he say what he wants to see me about?'

'No, he didn't. I guess policemen are naturally secretive about such things. It's too bad, too, because I'm curious to know. You obviously haven't done anything illegal today, so it must be something left over from last night, and I'm wondering how someone could get involved with the police on a night when nothing at all happened to him. Isn't that what you said?'

'If I said anything whatever, it was far too much. In the future, if you so much as ask me how I'm feeling, I'll plead the Fifth Amendment. Send Mr. McBride in.'

'It's Lieutenant McBride. That's what he said. He looks official, and so you'd better use his official title.'

'Thanks very much for the advice. Send him in.'

She withdrew her bright head with its bright, inquisitive eyes, and I thought how odd everyone becomes when anything sufficiently out of the ordinary happens. As a lawyer, it is not unusual for me to traffic moderately with the police, but now, because of what had happened last night to Beth, a call by a cop was suddenly something with all sorts of implications, and that's the way everyone becomes, the way Millie was — susceptible to exaggerated notions and given to exorbitant expectations.

As for me, I wasn't expecting very much, because Cotton McBride wasn't very much to expect. He must have been ten years older than I, but I had known him casually for a long time, since before the time he'd sent off to Chicago for his first mail-order course in private detecting, including fingerprint kit, and I think that he had changed less in appearance in all those years than anyone else I knew. He was thin and dry, with limp pale hair and round shoulders and a chronic expression of quiet despair, and he did not look much older now than he had twenty years ago. This was not because he kept himself looking young, but because I couldn't remember a time when he hadn't looked old. Even as a kid he had seemed dry and withered and a little tired, always wearing his expression of quiet despair. Wearing it now with a wilted seersucker suit and a black string tie, he made me think, as he came into the room, of an unsuccessful mortician.

'Hello, Cotton,' I said. 'Millie says I ought to call you lieutenant. She says you look official.'

'I heard her. That's a neat redhead, Gid, but she doesn't show much respect. An officer of the law is entitled to a little more respect, it seems to me.'

'I wouldn't take it too personally. She doesn't show much respect for me, either.'

'I judged that from the rest I heard. She shows a lot of other stuff, though, that probably makes up for it. That's a neat redhead, and I'm bound to admit it. You always had an eye for the lookers, Gid. I remember that about you.'

'Do you? Maybe so. It's not an uncommon post-puberty trait among males.'

'What I'd like to know is how you get

that little wife of yours to tolerate it. Seems to me that a wife wouldn't be very favorable to having a redhead like that around.'

'My wife's vain. She simply can't conceive of my looking twice at anyone but her.'

'A man would be a fool if he did. Even at the redhead. A man married to someone like that little wife of yours, I mean.' He sat down uninvited in a chair beside my desk, dropping his stained straw hat on the floor beside him. 'I never had any luck with the girls myself. Guys like you had all the luck.'

'Some of it bad, Cotton. Girls have a way of being bad luck at times.'

'That's true enough. A man in my business sees a lot of it. I've seen more than one man in bad trouble because some woman got him there. On the other hand, I've seen women in the same condition because of some man. Like the one who got herself killed out in Dreamer's Park last night. Beth Thatcher. Married for a while to Wilson Thatcher. But you know that better than almost anybody else. You heard about her getting killed, I suppose.'

'I heard.'

'Seems to me you used to know her pretty well, didn't you?'

'Pretty well.'

'That's what I thought. As I recall, that was one of the times your luck was bad. Or maybe it was good, after all. She was born to be trouble that one was. Maybe you were lucky out of it.'

'Maybe so. I'm happy enough with the way things have turned out.'

'They've turned out a lot better for you than they have for her, that's certain. Still, when you think back on it that was a pretty dirty trick she played on you. Something like that can sometimes do peculiar things to a fellow. It sticks. Maybe he thinks he's forgotten all about it, and then all at once something brings it back, and it's as bad as ever. Maybe worse.'

'Oh, for God's sake, Cotton. She got married and went away, and she was gone seven years. She quit being important quite a while back.'

'No, she didn't, Gid. She was killed last

night, and that makes her still important. Anyhow, it makes her important all over again. What I've been wondering is, why did she come back to town?'

'I can answer that. She had been living well in various places where living well is expensive, and she was broke. She needed some money, and she thought that Wilson Thatcher might be willing to give her some for old time's sake.'

'The hell she did! How do you know all this?'

'She told me so herself. I saw her yesterday evening in the Kiowa Room, as you probably know. We had a couple of gimlets apiece and talked about this and that. Nothing significant.'

'Isn't that just like a God damn crazy woman? What the hell would make her think Wilson Thatcher would just give her some money for the asking?'

'I told you. Old times' sake.'

'If you ask me, that's a hell of a poor reason for giving away money.'

'If I know Wilson Thatcher, he would agree with you.'

'Maybe you don't know him so well.

It's beginning to look to me like he might have thought it a reason good enough.'

'Is that so? Why?'

'Because you said she was broke, but she wasn't. Not when we checked her room at the hotel this morning. There was a purse of hers in the top drawer of a chest, and there was five grand in the purse. I thought it was a damn careless way to treat a bundle like that, but I guess you're naturally careless with things that come that easy.'

'What makes you think she got it from Wilson?'

'Who else? Did you give it to her?'

'Oh, sure. I've been paying her five grand a month for years. She was blackmailing me.'

'You're trying to be funny, I guess, but I'm always open to good suggestions, and you've made one that may not seem so bad after I've looked it over for a while.'

'Blackmail? Don't be a damn fool, Cotton.'

'I'll try not to be. It wasn't you I had in mind, though. Hell, I know you don't have the kind of money you need to pay blackmail. Wilson Thatcher's different. Wilson has most of the money in the world. You said what you said about her coming to ask him for some of it, and maybe that was just a nice way of putting it. I talked with Wilson this morning, but I've got a notion I'd better talk with him again.'

'Did Wilson see her before she died?'

'He says not. He says she called him out at the factory early yesterday afternoon and tried to make an appointment with him, but he told her to go to hell. She must have given old Wilson a pretty rough time out there in California. He had a bellyful. He hadn't heard about her being dead until I told him, but he didn't seem particularly surprised. That could be because he already knew without being told, though. What do you think?'

'You're the detective, Cotton. You do the thinking.'

'I've done plenty already, and I'll do plenty more. Don't you worry about that. Seems to me, however, that you might be willing to help. It might turn out to be in your own interest if you did.'

'What the hell do you mean by that?'

'It's plain enough. As far as anybody knows right now, there's as much reason for suspecting you as anyone else, and the quicker it turns out to be someone else, the better for you.'

'Oh, nuts. Is that what you came here to say? If it is, you've said it, and I want to go home.'

'You needn't get sore about it, Gid. As a detective, it's my business to figure that anyone might be guilty until it proves otherwise, and you ought to expect it. Why I really came is because you probably knew her better than anyone left around here, except maybe Wilson, and I thought you might know something that happened in the past that might help us now. Look at it this way. She came here to town yesterday morning on the train, and the night of the day she came she was killed out there in Dreamer's Park. The way that looks to me, she was sure as hell killed, for whatever reason, by someone right here in town, and probably you and I both know whoever it was.'

'Not necessarily. Someone could have followed her.'

'Not necessarily, sure, but most likely. There aren't any suspicious strangers in town that I know of. You know of any?'

'He could have come and gone. Murderers don't usually hang around after the murder.'

'It could have happened that way, and I won't say it couldn't have, but I don't believe it. What's bothering me right now as much as anything else is why she was out there in that park at night. It just doesn't seem like a reasonable place to be at night unless you're a kid after nooky, and she wasn't any kid, and she had a hotel room at her disposal besides.'

'She may have just walked out there for sentimental reasons. Dreamer's Park has played a part in most of our lives around here, Cotton, and Beth was actually a sentimental person in her own way, although it wasn't always apparent.'

'I don't believe that, either. It doesn't explain why she was killed there.'

'Assume a nut. There she was in the dark park for sentimental reasons, and there at the same time for reasons of his own was a psycho. It just happened.'

'That's possible, and it would probably be a big relief to someone if we bought it, but we don't. Not me, anyhow. For one thing, the killing was too neat. Nuts are generally messy. Whoever did this just slipped a long thin blade into her from behind, and that was all of it. The coroner says the blade reached the heart, and she probably died fast without ever knowing exactly what happened to her.'

I remembered her face in the light of a match, the fixed wonder that was almost an expression of serenity, and it was in that instant, for the first time since finding her dead in the old bandstand, that I realized fully that dying had not made her someone else with nothing to do with anything that had happened, and that she was still, although dead, the same person I had known and loved and ached for and wanted once to marry. I wasn't sorry now, after the temporary illusion of yesterday's sad evening, that she had made a jilted jackass of me, and in fact I was grateful that she had, since she had left, in leaving, a vacancy for Sid, but I was sorry for a lot of other things, and most of all I felt sorry and guilty for having agreed to meet her in the place where she was killed.

I had said that she had quit being important a long time ago, which was true in a way, but Cotton McBride had said that dying made her important all over again, which was also true in another way that wasn't the way that Cotton had meant. I wasn't quite sure of the way myself, but I suddenly hoped with all my heart, which was hurting, that someone even guiltier than I turned out to be even sorrier than I that she had died in the particular way that she had.

'What's the matter?' Cotton said.

'Nothing,' I said. 'Why?'

'You're looking funny.'

'Am I? I don't feel funny. Not by a damn sight. I was wondering what you've done with her.'

'The body? It's over in a back room of Paley's Funeral Parlor. The coroner's finished with it. Maybe Paley is too. You might be able to see it if you're interested.'

'Thanks. I might be interested. I'm also

interested in going home, Cotton, if you're agreeable. I was just getting ready to leave when you came in.'

'All right. I'm finished for now, I guess. You haven't been much help, to tell the truth. If you get any better ideas, you let me know.'

'I'll do that.'

He retrieved his stained hat and left, and I went out and told Millie to go home, or wherever she wanted to go, which she did willingly after being convinced that I hadn't been arrested. It was three-thirty then, and I returned to my office and stood by my desk looking down at the phone. Sid was home, organizing her notes on Zoroaster and waiting for me to call, and I wanted to call at once, without further delay for any reason, but I didn't. After a minute or two, I went out and downstairs and east on the street three blocks and two blocks south to Charlie Paley's Funeral Parlor. Excuse me. Chapel, he called it. There was a little chapel, all right, with an organ, and I had a fancy when I went in that I could hear 'Beautiful Isle of

Somewhere' coming out of the pipes, but actually the organ was silent and the chapel was empty. I found Charlie's office, Charlie in it, and he said it was all right to see Beth, she was ready, and he took me back to see her.

She was lying in this little room just off the alley, and it seemed to me a bleak and depressing room to lie in, even dead, but Beth didn't seem to mind, her face serene and still fixed in wonder, although it was now apparently the wonder of a dream, for her eyes were closed.

Charlie went away and left me with her, and I stood there and tried to say silently the proper goodbye that we had never said, but it was simply something that couldn't now be wrapped up neatly after being and ending in such disorder, and after a fair trial that came to nothing I went back to the Rexall drugstore across from my office and called Sid.

She said she was just getting ready to come, and I crossed the street and stood on the curb until she came, and we went home.

8

It was something like seven, thereabouts, and we were out on the back terrace in a couple of sling chairs, holding hands in one of those prolonged aftermaths, almost apathetically tender, which sometimes follow, assuming an appropriate pair, a busy and pleasurable time of greater intensity. The cicadas were up there in the trees, under which the shadows had a kind of blue transparency, and I was looking at the martin house on a tall pole at the rear of the yard, remembering how I used to lie on my back in a shady place for nearly a whole afternoon at a time in order to watch the slim birds gliding on still wings against the blue and white of sky and clouds. You may think that I had more immediate and significant things to think about, which I did, but they were things that I didn't *want* to think about, and so, as an evasion technique, I thought about other things more agreeable, including martins. As a matter of fact, all the afternoon since Sid had picked me up at the curb downtown had been devoted, from love to *Aves*, to the evasion of unpleasant reflections on death in general and a certain death in particular. In spite of my best efforts and the most effective distractions, however, I had found myself, now and then, standing again in the bleak and bare little room at the rear of Charlie Paley's Funeral Parlor.

'Sugar,' Sid said, 'hasn't it been a pleasant evening?'

'Yes, it has. It has been an evening to remember.'

'Including part of the afternoon.'

'True. Afternoon and evening alike.'

'It makes me happy when I am able to show you a good time.'

'You show me the best time of anybody. Nobody could possibly make a time half so good as you.'

'Really? Sugar, it's very nice of you to say so. I was wondering, though, if I had been entirely successful . . . For the past

119

half hour you've been silent and sad-looking. Are you becoming depressed about something?'

'I'm a little depressed, but not excessively under the circumstances.'

'I understand, sugar. You are certainly entitled to a little depression if anyone is. It may become worse, however, if you just continue keeping everything to yourself. The psychological consequences of something like that can sometimes be quite bad. What happens is, you break out with all sorts of nasty traits that nobody can understand but that are really the results of whatever it is you're keeping to yourself.'

'I surely wouldn't want that to happen to me.'

'Well, there's very little you can do about it, once you have repressed something long enough to cause the damage. It's much better to talk about things truthfully before it is too late. Besides, I'm dying of curiosity to know if anything special has developed. Has there?'

'Something has developed, all right, but

I don't know how special it is. Cotton McBride came to see me in the office this afternoon.'

'Cotton McBride? Isn't he that faded-looking little man who is some kind of policeman?'

'Yes. He's a detective, and that's a kind of policeman.'

'Why on earth did he come to see you in the office?'

'He thought maybe I could tell him something that would help him find whoever killed Beth.'

'That seems rather ridiculous to me. Why should he just assume that you could tell him anything of the sort?'

'Oh, he's simply working in the dark, I think. I used to know her pretty well, and he had a notion I might remember something about something or someone in the past that might be significant. As a matter of fact, it happened that I *was* able to tell him something that may help, although it wasn't from any farther in the past than yesterday.'

'What were you able to tell him?'

'Beth was broke. She came to town to

see Wilson Thatcher. She wanted him to give her some money to live on. She didn't see anything unreasonable in this, even though Wilson's married again, but, then, Beth was always assured that anyone would be happy to give her anything she wanted whenever she wanted it.'

'How do you know she was broke? Did she tell you so?'

'Yes. When we were having gimlets in the Kiowa Room.'

'Well, we mustn't dwell on that. It's too dangerous. I'd like to know, however, if Wilson gave her the money. In my opinion, he wouldn't have been such a fool.'

'In my opinion, you're right. Anyhow, Wilson said he didn't. He said he refused to see her when she asked him to. That's according to Cotton McBride. Cotton wasn't so sure about it, though.'

'Not so sure? Why not?'

'Because, as it turned out, Beth had five grand in her room at the hotel. Cotton found it when he searched the room this morning.'

'Five thousand dollars? That's quite a lot of money for someone to have suddenly just after being broke.'

'Not so much for someone who liked to live well in places where living well was expensive. I've been thinking about it, and I'm sure it wasn't nearly as much as the amount Beth had in mind.'

'Nevertheless, it's quite a bit of money to most people, including Wilson Thatcher. He may have more money than is decent, which he does, but I've never known him to display exceptional generosity when it comes to giving any of it away, and I'm willing to bet two to one that he didn't voluntarily give any to an ex-wife for nothing more than the asking.'

'I'm inclined to agree. So is Cotton.'

'Do you think he gave it to her because she forced him in one way or another?'

'This is one line of reasoning that seems indicated.'

'It's absolutely fascinating, isn't it? What do you suppose Wilson could have done to make him susceptible?'

'I can't imagine. It wouldn't surprise me to learn that he cheats on his income tax, but I can't see him doing anything really juicy.'

'You never can tell, however. Wilson Thatcher may not have always acted like a deacon just because he looks like one. Suppose he did something once that he doesn't want known, and your precious Beth tried to blackmail him because of it. Wouldn't that be an acceptable reason for his killing her if it could be proved?'

'Acceptable, indeed. I can detect a couple of flaws in the supposition, though. In the first place, why pay her five grand and kill her afterward? Why not kill her before and keep the five grand in the bank?'

'Perhaps he felt compelled to give her the money as a kind of down payment or something until he could get her in a position to do what he wanted to her.'

'I concede the possibility, but I have no faith in it. Flaw number two, in my judgment, is even more critical. In spite of the precedent of the commissioner and the mayor's elderly sister, I consider it extremely unlikely that Wilson deviated from propriety a sufficient degree to make him a subject for blackmail. Having known him and Beth both from away back, I'm satisfied that the deviations, whatever they may have been, were on the distaff side. The view is supported by the nature of their divorce. Wilson, as you pointed out, is only slightly poorer than Croesus and could have been tapped for a steady increment of magnificent proportions if he had been vulnerable. Nothing like this happened, however. A settlement was made quietly, and Beth went off quietly for her divorce. A few years later, she turns up broke. I submit that any major diversion by Wilson, felonious or merely scandalous, would have kept her living well in Miami and Rio and Acapulco and places like that indefinitely.'

'At any rate, you clearly admit that she was not above blackmailing him, which is very enlightening, to say the least, and I must say that you certainly picked a sweet bitch in your first heat.'

I thought about this, about trying to explain it, but I knew it would be hopeless, besides being disastrous, and so I didn't try. How can you possibly hope to explain someone who could surely have made blackmail seem like an amiable and reasonable negotiation, conducted without malice in the friendliest fashion with the most sincere wish for no hard feelings? That was the way Beth had surely done it, if she did it at all, but I didn't think she had for the reasons I cited to Sid. I was silent for quite a while, having nothing convincing or even safe to say, and after quite another while Sid said something more.

'Never mind, sugar,' she said. 'It's not fair of me to be so critical, for everyone understands that men don't know any more about women than what's used for what, and I'm only interested in protecting you from the consequences of your foolishness, whether it was seven years ago or last night. Did Cotton McBride have any notion that you went to Dreamer's Park?'

'I don't think so. I'm sure he didn't. Why should he?'

'Do you think it would make things difficult for you if he found out about it?'

'I think it would.'

'In that case, we must be prepared to lie about it convincingly if necessary, and we had better agree at once on the lies we will tell. It wouldn't do at all for one of us to say one thing while the other was saying something else.'

'I can see that it wouldn't make a particularly favorable impression. I'm wondering, though, if it might not be better to tell the truth.'

'Certainly not. Put any such nonsense right out of your head. The truth is so ridiculous that even I, as you will recall, had difficulty in believing it, and I have no doubt that the police would find it absolutely impossible. They'd clap you right into jail without hesitation. Besides, you've waited far too long. If you were going to tell about going to Dreamer's Park, you should have told immediately. At this point, you could hardly avoid an effect of duplicity, to say nothing of positive imbecility.'

'Thanks.'

'We have to be realistic, sugar. Although I'm your wife and in love with you and all that, I'm bound to say that you haven't been especially brilliant in this matter. You had better consider my opinions carefully if you want to escape some unpleasant consequences, and it's my opinion that we must lie, if necessary, to keep you from becoming more involved than you already are.'

'It may be a problem in a pinch to make a good story stick. After all, you were with Rose Pogue discussing Zoroaster, so you can hardly go on record as being with me, and I was alone all the time, which is impossible to prove.'

'Don't be dull, sugar. As a lawyer, you surely realize that you don't have to prove that you weren't in Dreamer's Park. It will be entirely up to the police to prove that you were. All you have to do is repeat earnestly that you were at home all the time, and I'll insist that you were here when I returned, which happens to be the truth and no lie at all.'

She made it sound remarkably simple and sensible and even honorable, as if candor and deceit had somehow exchanged places in the scale of values, and I was diagnosing this with the intent of further discussion when there was suddenly a soft, dry sound from a rear corner of the house behind us, and I turned my head and looked back there to see who or what had made the sound, and it was no one but Wilson Thatcher who had made it by coughing to attract our attention. I stood up with a funny feeling to face him, and he came across from the house to the terrace with a long-legged stride that appeared to be a kind of slow-motion lope.

Sid had said that he looked like a deacon, although possibly not always acting like one, and I guess that's what he looked like, if a deacon is tall and thin with lank black hair and a dyspeptic face with pale blue eyes tending to project.

Actually, he was not a bad fellow, pleasant enough most of the time, and I'd always rather liked him in an unenthusiastic way, even though our associations, such as they were, had been somewhat strained for reasons stated. Right now, he looked uncertain and apologetic, holding one hand in an odd position before his mouth, as if he were keeping prepared to cover another cough. I thought to myself, watching him approach, that he had surely been no match for Beth, who had surely given him a bad time while it lasted, and I felt sorry for him all at once and hoped that his trouble, if he had any, was no worse than mine, which might be bad enough.

'Hello, Wilson,' I said. 'Glad to see you.'

This wasn't quite true. It was true that I was curious, but I wasn't really glad, and I was prepared, in fact, to be the contrary. He held out a dry hand, which I took and released, and he looked over my shoulder at Sid, who had risen and turned, and relaxed his face briefly in a thin, dyspeptic smile.

'I rang at the front door,' he said, 'but no one answered, and so I took the liberty of walking around the house. I hope I'm not intruding.'

'Not at all. Come over and sit down.'

'Thanks, Gideon.' He stood for a moment with an air of abstraction, staring off into the dusky yard and popping his knuckles by flexing his fingers, and then he moved over to a chair and stood beside it politely, waiting for Sid to sit down again before sitting down himself.

'Perhaps I should have waited and come to your office tomorrow, but what I want to talk about is rather urgent and delicate. I preferred coming here, if you don't mind.'

'You're welcome to come,' Sid said, 'but I don't intend to leave, however delicate whatever you have to say may be.'

'No, no.' Wilson did not seem surprised or distressed by Sid's blunt statement of position, and I could hear the soft popping of knuckles, one, two, three, four, as he folded into his chair in a kind of boneless surrender to it. 'Since I've invaded the privacy of your home, so to speak, you are both perfectly within your rights to hear what I have to say.'

We waited for him to begin saying it, and after another brief interval of soft popping sounds, he did.

'The truth is,' he said, 'I'm afraid I may need a lawyer.'

'You already have several lawyers,' I said. 'What do you need with another?'

'Company lawyers. They're all right for

business matters, but this is something different. Personal. To be frank, I've committed an indiscretion that may prove extremely troublesome. It has put me, I confess, in a difficult position.'

I wondered if he was referring to murder, the slipping of a long, thin blade into Beth from behind, and I thought that indiscretion, if that was what he meant, was a discreet word for it.

'Indiscretions sometimes have a way of proving troublesome,' I said.

'Yes,' said Sid, 'don't they!'

'My indiscretion,' Wilson said, 'was the telling of a lie.'

'That's very interesting,' Sid said. 'We were discussing the telling of lies as a matter of prudence just before you came.'

'A lie,' I said, 'is scarcely a legal problem unless it was told under oath.'

'It wasn't told under oath,' Wilson said, 'but it was told to the police, which is the next thing to it. I told it to Cotton McBride, to be exact, and now I've been compelled to retract it as a result of a later development, and my position has become, as I said, difficult if not precarious.'

'Maybe you'd better tell me directly what it's all about,' I said. 'That is, if you're serious about wanting my opinion. Not that I'd recommend me under the circumstances. I may need a lawyer myself pretty soon.'

'I'd be grateful if you'd listen to me. I shouldn't blame you, however, if you refused. You may have guessed that it concerns someone we have both known quite well.'

'Beth, you mean. I've guessed.'

'Yes. Yes, of course.' He cleared his throat and popped knuckles. 'I've been told that you saw her and talked with her at the Carson yesterday.'

'That's right. She told me she had come to town to see if you would give her some money. She said she was broke.'

'She told you that? Beth was an incredible person. I was never able to understand her at all. I can't imagine any other woman on earth who would openly imply that she was attempting blackmail.'

'Did you say blackmail?'

'Well, that wasn't what Beth called it, and I really doubt that she recognized it

133

as such, but you can't call it anything else if you want to be realistic. You know how Beth was. She had a marvelous capacity for rationalization, and a genuine belief in euphemisms. Anything was what you called it. She was perfectly agreeable, absolutely without any apparent malice, and she was surprised and hurt to discover that I was not anxious to give her twenty thousand dollars. I'm sure she thought I was unreasonable and parsimonious to protest.'

Sid made a derisive sound, but I made no sound at all for several seconds, because I believed what he said was true, and I was trying to understand why in the devil he had said it, to me or to anyone, for it gave him a motive for murder that even Cotton McBride could appreciate, and it had much better been left unsaid so far as I could see.

'Twenty thousand dollars is a lot of money,' I said. 'It ought to pay for a pretty big mistake.'

'It wasn't anything I did deliberately.' Wilson sighed and seemed to sag a little more in his chair, and I found myself feeling for him again the sympathy and strange liking that I had felt before, in spite of what he had once done to me, which really hadn't been deliberate either. 'In fact, it wasn't anything I did at all. I was simply stupid, that's what I was, and I suppose stupidity is always expensive. You remember when Beth and I separated out in California? Well, of course you do. You also remember that we settled things amicably between us out of court. I made a very generous settlement, it seems to me, for I don't mind telling you that I could have gotten off without paying her a penny. Not a single penny. It would have entailed a lot of unpleasantness, however, and I was glad enough to settle.

'Anyhow, she took what I gave her and went off to get a divorce, which was part of our understanding. Soon after she left, I came back here to manage the main factory, and later on I got notice from her that the divorce had been granted. In a couple of years, I married again, and everything seemed to be satisfactorily settled and almost forgotten until Beth showed up here yesterday and told me

135

that I was a bigamist.'

'A *what*?'

'A bigamist. A man with more than one wife at the same time. She said she hadn't ever actually gotten a divorce. She intended to at first, but somehow she kept putting it off, and finally she decided it would be unnecessary to get one at all. She hadn't meant to cause me any inconvenience or trouble, but it wasn't really much of a problem, after all, for she was willing to go away quietly again, and all that was required of me was to give her twenty thousand dollars to go on.'

'Didn't you sign any divorce papers or anything, for God's sake?'

'Yes, I did, but she said they were phony. She had them drawn up by a disbarred lawyer she met somewhere, because, she said, being married made her feel a little more secure in case something came up to make a husband handy. I should have had my lawyers check it out, of course, but I guess it just didn't occur to me seriously that she might do something like that. It looked perfectly in order and all, but I admit that

I know practically nothing about such matters. I admitted in the beginning that I was stupid.'

'I hope you haven't been stupid enough to tell all this to anyone else.'

'That's what I wanted to talk with you about. I told Cotton McBride that I refused to see Beth, but then he found the five thousand dollars in her room, and later I had to admit that I'd seen her and given her the money, because he was sure to find it out one way or another, and it would only have looked worse for me if I kept on lying. I still didn't quite tell the truth, though, not all of it, for I merely said I gave her the money because she needed it. I didn't say anything about my being a bigamist, or blackmail, or that the five thousand, which was all I had in my office safe, was only an initial payment on twenty. Now I'm afraid it will all come out sooner or later in the investigation of what happened to Beth last night, and I'm wondering if it wouldn't be better to tell it voluntarily in my own way.'

'Do you realize the probable consequences if you do?'

'Yes. I'll be suspected of killing her. I may even be arrested, and I suppose I must be prepared to face it. It's odd, isn't it, how something like this can develop all of a sudden with no warning whatever?' He got up abruptly from his chair with an unfolding motion and stood looking into the darkening yard, and I could hear once more that soft, measured popping of knuckles.

'It was damn inconsiderate of Beth to let me go on thinking I was divorced, getting married again and all, but it was even more inconsiderate to come back here and get herself killed the way she did. Still, you know, I can't seem to feel any malice toward her for it. I can't even feel that she really meant me any harm. Maybe you'll understand that. I don't know. I always thought a lot of Beth. I kept wishing that she'd change enough so that things could go on between us, but she didn't, and they couldn't, and now I wish that things had turned out better for her than they did, but there's no use in wishing to change what is over and done with. Her father died when she was a young girl, you know, and her mother died several years ago, while Beth and I were in California. Do you happen to know if there are any other relatives living?'

'I don't think so. None who would care or concern themselves.'

'Well, she must be buried, of course, and I guess I'm the logical one to see that it's done in good order. I'll buy a little place for her in the cemetery and make the arrangements. It can be done quite simply and cheaply, I think. There's no sense in making a great fuss about it.'

Sid and I had both stood up with him, and now he suddenly made a jerky half-turn toward us and an odd little half-bow from the waist that somehow managed to give an effect of great courtliness.

'Thank you for tolerating my intrusion. It's been a relief to talk to someone, but I'll have to decide for myself, after all, what I must do. I won't ask you to treat this as a privileged communication if you feel that you shouldn't. Now I'll say good night.'

He completed his turn, now away from us, and walked over to the house and out of sight around the corner. There was a kind of lanky, loping dignity about him that was pretty touching, and he was quite a puzzlement besides.

'I wonder why he really came here,' I said, 'and I wonder why he told us what he did. I can't see any sense in it. If Beth tricked him about the divorce and made a bigamist of him, it seems to me that the sensible thing would simply have been to keep quiet about it, and chances are, now that Beth's dead, that no one would ever have known. Some people can't live peacefully alone with something like that on their mind, however. They just have to get rid of it by talking, and maybe Wilson's one of them. It's a kind of catharsis.'

'Well,' said Sid, 'I'm most relieved to know that there is a fatter suspect in this business than you, and I'm pleased, moreover, to discover that he has behaved, all in all, with even less intelligence. It's very encouraging.'

'He seemed sad and confused,' I said. 'I

felt sorry for him.'

'If he had popped his God damn knuckles one more time,' Sid said, 'I'd surely have screamed.'

9

On Saturday we buried Beth. Charlie
Paley moved her up from the rear room
to the chapel for the occasion, and I don't
think it took more than twenty minutes to
get the service finished from first to last.
There was a minister who said a few
words about hope everlasting, which I
had heard before with minor variations,
and a semipro tenor about town sang a
song with organ accompaniment, and the
song he sang was 'Somewhere the Sun Is
Shining'.

Well, it was shining right outside,
although not for Beth, and after the
service I drove out in it to the cemetery.
Sid was with me, and maybe a dozen
other people in other cars. Wilson
Thatcher was there, but not his wife, and
Cotton McBride was there, and so was
Sara Pike. The others were people who
had known her and may have been sorry
that she was dead, and we all gathered

around the fresh grave in the little place that Wilson had provided. It was in a corner of the cemetery where the graves came to an end, and just across a fence there was a field full of white clover. A locust tree cast a pattern of light shade on the clipped grass and turned earth, and altogether it was as pretty a place as one could wish to be dead in, although I'm sure Beth wouldn't have wished, if she could have, to be dead in any place whatever.

Sid stood beside me and held my hand, and when it was all over we turned and left. I still didn't feel, walking away, that I had said goodbye to anyone, or that I had finished anything that needed finishing. What I felt was at odds ends, the strange disconsolate sense of leaving undone what I would never get back to do. Sid and I had not spoken since leaving Charlie Paley's Chapel, and we didn't speak now until we had left the cemetery and were back into town. Then she asked me if there was anything I especially wanted to do, and I said I especially wanted to go home.

'I thought you might feel like going somewhere and doing something,' she said.

'Home is somewhere,' I said, 'and anything I want to do can be done there.'

'Do you have anything particular in mind?'

'Yes, I do. I have it in mind to mow the yard.'

'That's a rather odd thing to want particularly to do. Why do you?'

'There are several reasons. For one thing, I find mowing the yard a comfort. It is almost mathematically neat, and you can always measure so exactly what is left to be done by what has been done already. For another thing, the grass is getting high. Finally, mowing is a domestic task, and I'm feeling domestic. It's a kind of recession, I think. A need for sanctuary. A modified retreat to the womb. Only the other evening I was wanting to live in a jungle or on a beach or corruptly in someplace like Paris, but now Hoolihan's Addition suits me fine as a place to live and someday die. Provided, of course that you agree to live there with me and let me die first.'

'I don't know about that. I may insist upon dying first myself. I don't believe I'd care much for Hoolihan's Addition as a place to live alone.'

'Never mind. The decision may not be left in our hands, and so there is no need for us to disagree about it. I don't want to disagree with anybody about anything. All I want to do is mow the yard and be domestic.'

'Now that you've made such a case for it, I feel inclined to be domestic too. You have made it sound delightful.'

'Aren't you afraid being domestic will make you feel like a wife?'

'Not necessarily. It's a matter of attitude and inner control. One may feel like a wife at a spring dance and like a mistress in the kitchen. You only need a little ingenuity.'

'I'd say that ingenuity is something you have more than a little of. I've noticed it more than once. What particular form is your domesticity going to take?'

'In order to keep you company, I plan to do something outside. Perhaps I could clip around the edges of things while you're mowing.'

'Good. That will be constructive, as well as domestic, and I'll appreciate the company.'

We rode along silently until we turned onto our street and approached our drive. Sid was sitting with her legs folded under her and her nylon knees showing below the skirt of the plain black dress she had worn in deference to a funeral, and I could see from the corners of my eyes that she looked, in silence, sad and pensive.

'She looked much younger than I thought she would,' she said suddenly. 'What happened is just too damn bad.'

'Yes, it is,' I said. 'It's just too bad.'

I turned into the drive and stopped, and we got out and went into the house together. Sid peeled off toward the kitchen with a cool drink of something in mind, and I climbed the stairs to our room and changed from the light worsted I was wearing to an old pair of denims cut off above the knees in imitation of Bermuda shorts. With these I wore a seasoned T-shirt and a pair of loafers with part of the heels remaining, and the effect was comfortable if not fashionable. In my opinion, half the fun of being domestic is in looking disreputable, like a bum, and I've often defended this opinion against Sid, who does not share it. She tolerates it, however, Sid being in most matters a tolerant person, and I have even suspected her of secretly approving it, in spite of what she says, for she is mildly disreputable herself in more respects than a few.

And so, looking disreputable, like a bum, I went downstairs and into the garage and started the power mower and began to mow the front yard. It was a fairly deep yard from street to house, and you could get a pretty free and easy feeling of being in the stretch every time you made a turn and started from one to the other. I took my time, because it was a hot day and I was in no hurry, and I had only cut about a quarter of the yard, working from one side toward the center, when Sid came out to clip around edges. She was wearing cotton gloves and short shorts, and she waved at me with her clippers from a distance as if she had not seen me for a long time and was surprised and delighted to see me now. She began clipping along the brick border of a flower bed in front of the house, and she looked altogether charming and distracting, but not at all domestic.

I kept right at it until I had finished the front yard, after which I cut the narrow stretch beside the house on the east and then went on into the back. It was a hot day, as I said, very hot in the sun and not much less so in the shade, and by this time my T-shirt was soaked and my mouth was full of cotton. After a couple of times to the alley and back, I killed the engine under a tree with the idea of going into the kitchen for something cold and wet, but then I saw Sid coming out of the house and across the yard with two cans of Schlitz, which met the specifications perfectly, and so I sat down with my back against the tree and waited for Sid to come on with the beer and sit down beside me.

We sat there in domesticated contentment under the tree, flank to flank and drinking the cold beer slowly, and it was by way of being a pretty good time after some bad ones until Cotton McBride appeared at the side of the house and came on back to where we were. If it had been necessary at the moment to name the last person in the world I wanted to see, it might not have been Cotton that I named, but he would surely have been in contention.

There, however, he was, last or next to last, and I thought under the circumstances that I had better be polite.

'Hello, Cotton,' I said. 'It's a hot day.'

'Ninety-eight in the sun,' Cotton said. 'I see you've been mowing the yard.'

'I've been mowing and Sid's been clipping. We stopped to have a beer.'

'How are you, Mrs. Jones? Those beers look mighty inviting, I'll tell you that. If I wasn't on duty, I might have a good cold beer myself.'

'I shouldn't think one beer would interfere a great deal with your duty,' Sid said. 'My experience has been that one beer doesn't interfere with much of anything.'

'Come on and have one, Cotton,' I

said. 'It'll do you good.'

'Well, I shouldn't, it being against regulations and all, but I may have one at that. Thanks.'

'I'll go get it and be right back,' Sid said.

'What I came out for, Gid,' Cotton said, 'was to have a private talk about something important.'

'Let me tell you something,' Sid said. 'There isn't going to be any private talk that doesn't include me as one of the private parties, and so you may as well get any notion to the contrary out of your head.'

'I don't know about that,' Cotton said. 'You can't be intruding on police business, Mrs. Jones.'

'If it's police business, you had better, in my opinion, be conducting it in a police station, or somewhere besides my backyard.'

'That could be arranged, I guess, if you insist on it.'

'What do you mean, arranged? Are you threatening to arrest Gid? Is that what you mean?'

'I didn't intend to arrest him. Not yet, anyhow.'

'Not yet? Is that what you said? Not yet?'

'Sid,' I said, 'go get Cotton a beer, for God's sake.'

'I'm not at all sure that I care to give him a beer now,' Sid said. 'You may give a beer to someone who is threatening to arrest you if you choose, but I'm not quite so charitable.'

'Oh, come on. Please don't be unreasonable. Cotton's only doing his duty as he sees it.'

'It's a peculiar way to see it, if you ask me. There's no excuse that I can see for accepting someone's beer and hospitality with one breath and threatening to arrest him with the next.'

'Never mind the beer,' Cotton said. 'I don't believe I want one after all.'

'Of course you do,' I said. 'I'm about through with mine, and I'll have another one with you. Go get the beers, Sid, please.'

'I'll go only on condition that I'm included in the private talk,' Sid said.

'How about it, Cotton?' I said. 'Can Sid be included?'

'I guess it won't do any harm,' Cotton said, 'although I can't imagine that it will do any good, either.'

'In that case,' Sid said, 'I'll go.'

She stood up and tugged at her short shorts and started for the house, and Cotton sank down onto the grass and took off his stained straw hat, exposing pale limp hair plastered damply to his skull. He sat there in a wilted heap with his legs crossed before him at the ankles.

'That's a remarkable little woman,' he said. 'I don't know that I've ever seen a woman so determined about something that she didn't even know anything about.'

'Her deepest female instincts have been aroused. She's fighting for her mate.'

'Why the hell did she have to pick me to fight with? I haven't done anything to her mate. Not yet.'

'There's that ominous appendage again. Not yet. I agree with Sid that there seems to be a suspicion of threat in it.'

'Maybe so. I may know a few things I'm not talking about.'

'Oh? Shall I call my lawyer?'

The screen door banged at that instant, and Sid came back with the beers. She passed one to Cotton and one to me and sat down with the other.

'What has been said while I was gone?' she said.

'Nothing of importance,' I said.

'We were waiting to include you,' Cotton said.

'Then there's no sense in waiting any longer, since I'm here.'

'No, there isn't.' Cotton had been looking at Sid's brown legs, but now he took a swallow of beer and began looking at me.

'You remember what I told you in your office? How Wilson Thatcher denied seeing Beth or giving her any money?'

'I remember. You said you were going to talk to him again.'

'Well, I talked to him, all right, and in my judgment he told me a damn lie.'

'Does he still claim he didn't see Beth or give her the money?'

'No. Just the other way around. He claims he lied the first time about not seeing her, because he thought it might incriminate him or something, but he changed his mind and decided to tell the truth, and the truth is, according to him, that she called him out at the factory, and he arranged to meet her and give her the five grand.'

'Where did he meet her?'

'He says he picked her up on a corner, and they just drove around a few minutes, and then he let her out on the same corner, but as I said, I've got a notion it's a damn lie.'

'What makes you think so?'

'Hell, I just can't see any good reason why he should give her five grand if he was going to kill her afterward. Besides being a waste of money, which isn't like Wilson, it would make us think of him first thing.'

'You think he was telling the truth the first time and lying the second?'

'Damned if I know what I think, to tell the truth. It's all mixed up. Assuming that he did give her the money, why the hell should he tell us about it?'

'Because he's not a fool and assumes that you aren't either.'

'Which could easily be a mistake,' Sid said.

'Thanks,' Cotton said, ignoring Sid and concentrating on me. 'Maybe you wouldn't mind developing that a little.'

'Well, it's your position that he would never have given her the money and then killed her afterward, and it's my position that Wilson was perfectly capable of anticipating this. If you look at it this way, the fact that he gave her the money, if it *is* a fact, is the best evidence of his innocence.'

'You think so? I might agree if it wasn't for something else that I know and you don't.' He paused and swallowed more beer and looked at me for a few seconds with a sly expression in which there was a touch of smugness. 'Did you know Wilson Thatcher was a bigamist?'

This was clearly intended to be a bomb, which it had been at the time Wilson exploded it on the back terrace, but now it barely popped, and I had trouble in looking as incredulous as circumstances demanded. The only element of shock, so far as I was concerned, was that Wilson had been so rash as to spill his insides without restraint.

'Oh, cut it out,' I said. 'That's the most ridiculous thing I've ever heard.'

'It's a fact just the same. At least Wilson says it is, and I can't see why a man would say something like that about himself unless it was true.'

'By God, I can't see why he'd say it at all, true or otherwise.'

'He was afraid we'd find it out ourselves, and then it would look all the worse because he hadn't told. He didn't even know it himself until Beth Thatcher came to town and that's why she came. To tell him she'd never really gotten the divorce he thought she had, and to put the squeeze on him. The five grand, Wilson says, was just a down payment on twenty, and he was going to get the rest of it for her the next day. There's a couple of pretty good motives for murder, if you ask me. You kill one person and get rid of a wife who makes you a bigamist while you're saving fifteen good grand that would otherwise have to go after five bad.'

'Oh, sure, Cotton. Two wonderful motives. And so he just handed them to you out of pure charity and a natural desire to be hanged.'

'All right, Gid. You don't have to go on with it. It looks like the guy's going out of his way to make trouble for himself, and that's what bothers me. Fact is, I'm wondering why the hell he doesn't just confess to the murder and be done with it. He doesn't, though. He swears he never saw her again after paying the five grand, but I'm still not convinced that he actually paid her anything at all. Damn it, he didn't have to make any down payment, like he said, and it doesn't seem reasonable that he would have done it unless he honestly planned to give her the rest later. In that case he might have done it, because it wouldn't have made any difference one way or another.

'If he intended to kill her, though, he would've simply put her off until the next day for the full amount. It would've been easy enough to do, and as I've said before, he wouldn't have had the money turning up later to suggest a blackmail motive. Besides, what the hell kind of a reason for killing someone is this bigamy business? Or even for paying blackmail? It wasn't deliberate, and he could have proved it. He could even have proved that Beth had tricked him into it by a kind of fraud or something, which would have put her in a hell of a lot more trouble than he was in. The most it would have meant to him in the end, I suspect, was a little scandal and humiliation and the inconvenience of getting his second marriage legalized. I can maybe see a rich man laying out a bundle to avoid a scandal and all, but I'm damned if I can see him committing murder over it. Not if he's got any brains whatever, which Wilson Thatcher has.'

'Speaking of brains,' Sid said, 'you have almost convinced me that you may have some yourself.'

'What's that?' Cotton said.

'Well,' Sid said, 'you have obviously thought everything through, and weighed one thing against another, and come up finally with all these brilliant deductions and everything, and it seems to me that this requires a certain amount of brains, however inadequate.'

'It's kind of you to say so,' Cotton said. His ears had turned red, and I could see that he was somewhat hotter than the hot day. 'Thanks very much for the compliment, however inadequate.'

'You're welcome, I'm sure,' Sid said. 'I don't agree, however, that your final conclusion regarding Wilson Thatcher is sound. The weight of evidence surely indicates that he is sadly deficient in brains, if not totally without them. He has certainly talked like an idiot, saying first one thing and then another, and I consider it likely that he may have acted like one. For the purpose of being compatible, however, I'll concede that he must have had the glimmering of intelligence required to keep him from getting into a great sweat over the silly bigamy business, but I can tell you another person who would have got into the greatest sweat imaginable, even if she had all the brains in the world, and the person I mean, if you want to know, is no one but *Mrs.* Wilson Thatcher.'

Cotton was looking at her with his mouth open and so was I, even though I knew her somewhat better than Cotton and shouldn't have been particularly surprised by what was comparable to what had often happened before. Finally Cotton drained his can of beer and then began to read the label, at least the big print, as if it were something instructive or comforting, possibly a short prayer.

'Now what in hell, exactly,' he said, 'made you say that?'

'What made me say it,' she said, 'is being a woman with a husband, and I don't mind admitting that I would be considerably upset, to put it mildly, if another woman came along suddenly and told me that he had been her husband first and still was. Moreover, if this happened to be the result of a deliberate damn dirty trick, I'm sure I would try my best to make her sorry or dead. Women are more inclined to be sensitive to deceit and humiliation than men are, especially if they are practiced and imposed on by another woman. Although I have more brains than I need, and am not given to behaving as if I needed more than I have, I'm bound to say that my own reaction would be more emotional than intelligent in such a case.'

Cotton was still reading the label, forming with his lips the shapes of the words. He did this silently, his expression rather imbecilic, but I could tell that he was listening intently and thinking as furiously as his inadequate brains permitted.

'There's something else I'll tell you, if you care to listen,' Sid said.

'I don't believe I care to,' I said.

'As for me,' Cotton said, 'I'm listening.'

'It is apparent to anyone who has ever taken the trouble to consider it,' Sid said, 'that someone who is emotional about something is also vulnerable and likely to be more susceptible to threats than someone who isn't, and if I were married to a man who was also married to someone else, and if I wanted to make a good thing of it in the way of getting some money, I'd surely give serious consideration to the woman as the one to get it from. What I mean is, there is a good chance in my opinion that the man would simply tell me to go fly a kite or something, especially if he happened to be perfectly innocent so far as his intentions went, but you might be surprised to know how absolutely neurotic a woman who thought she was a legal wife would feel about having it known by everybody that she was really an illegal one and had been sleeping practically publicly with someone else's husband. She would feel a perfect fool, which is the worst way a woman can possibly feel. Or maybe there's no such thing as an illegal wife. Is there? Maybe she would simply not be a wife at all.'

'As a lawyer,' I said, 'I decline to give an opinion without consulting a lawyer.'

Cotton turned his beer can, now empty, around and around in his hands. He seemed to be trying to find his place among the words, which he had apparently lost. Suddenly, giving it up, he laid the can gently in the grass and got onto his knees and then to his feet. He stood looking for a few seconds over our heads toward a redbud tree at the rear of the yard.

'By God,' he said. 'Oh, by God.'

Turning without another word, he walked away and around the house and out of sight.

'What the hell's the matter with him?' Sid said. 'Is he mad or something?'

'I don't think he's mad,' I said. 'I think he's just a little disturbed.'

'What about? Because I tried to get him to consider things reasonably?'

'That might be it. I've got a notion you made quite an impression.'

'It was damn impolite of him, if you ask me, not even to thank us for the beer.'

'He didn't intend to be impolite. He was abstracted. Stunned may be the word.'

'Oh, nonsense. I only pointed out a few things he should have thought of himself. I wonder why he didn't?'

'That's what he's wondering. Anyhow, you were admirable and irresistible. I want to congratulate you.'

'It isn't necessary to congratulate me

for not being an idiot.'

'True. Nevertheless, it was a deft job of directing suspicion on a woman who is probably as innocent as you are.'

'Well, if she's innocent, it will do her no harm in the end, and I'm convinced that it will be favorable to our own cause. In order to keep you out of jail, if possible, we must have as many suspects as can be arranged.'

'I see. Sort of a calculated confusion. Well, as Voltaire said, let us tend our garden. To be more precise, let us finish the yard.'

'I don't believe I'll clip around any more edges. I'm rather tired of it.'

'I sympathize. Clipping is not a job to sustain one's interest very long.'

I got up and started the mower and finished mowing the backyard, and Sid sat under the tree and watched me do it.

10

It was raining when I woke the next morning, the morning of Sunday, and it rained gently without stopping until about five o'clock in the afternoon, and in the meanwhile, between waking and five, it was a quiet and undemanding day that Sid and I spent pleasantly in various ways without intrusions. After the rain stopped, between five and six, we considered going out somewhere to get something to eat, but we decided that going out was something we didn't particularly want to do, having had a pretty good time staying in, and so we found some cold chicken in the refrigerator, which we ate at the kitchen table with bread and butter and beer.

It was clearing and cool outside after the rain, and we went out onto the back terrace before dark and sat there while darkness came, and the stars were out among what was left of the clouds. I went to sleep in my chair and woke up after ten, almost eleven, and Sid was asleep in her chair beside me. I woke her, and we went inside and had a drink and went to bed and to sleep after a while. What I'm trying to say is that it was a good day of its kind, and I was glad to have it to remember later, for the next one was bad.

It started out all right, a brisk walk to the office and Millie already there in a good humor with her bright head cocked like a woodpecker's, and it stayed all right, if not exceptional, until mid-morning, which was about the time that Millie took a call from the county attorney, who wanted to talk to me. The county attorney's name was Hector Caldwell. We were about the same age, and he had always been a friend of mine, which he was still, so far as I knew, but he was compelled in his professional capacity, as it turned out, to treat me in an unfriendly fashion.

When Millie announced who it was wanted to talk to me, I took up the phone and said, 'Hello, Hec,' and he said, 'Hello, Gid,' and I said, 'What can I do for you?'

and he said, 'I wonder if you could get over to my office right away,' and I said, 'Well, I don't think I can make it right away,' and he said, 'I think maybe you'd better,' and I knew in an instant, although his voice was pleasant, that I damn well had no choice one way or the other. I did have the alternative of leaving town in a hurry, of course, but the alternative did not appeal to me, hurried or not, and so I left my office on the way to Hec's and was almost to the hall when Millie stopped me. 'You be careful what you say to that Hector Caldwell,' she said.

'You've been listening on the extension again,' I said.

'Don't admit anything,' she said.

'What the hell are you talking about?'

'I don't trust that son of a bitch. He wants to be governor or something someday.'

'You're just a crazy redhead. What the hell makes you think I've got anything to admit?'

'I don't think you necessarily have, although I wouldn't bet on it, but I think *he* thinks you have, and I could tell by the snotty tone of his voice.'

'Snotty? It sounded normal enough to me, except possibly right at the end.'

'Well, it's normally snotty, that's why, but it's right at the end that I'm mainly talking about. Who the hell does he think he is to be ordering you around?'

'He thinks he's the county attorney, that's who, and I think you'd better quit listening in on my telephone conversations. Don't you have any sense of shame at all?'

'It isn't nearly as keen as my sense of trouble, and the trouble I sense is something you're in, whatever it may be precisely. Maybe you shouldn't go talk to that Hector Caldwell at all. I'll let you hide out in my apartment if you want to.'

'The invitation suggests certain intriguing possibilities, but I'll have to decline. When I married Sid, she made me promise to give up staying with other girls in their apartments. She's unreasonable about such trifles.'

'I was only trying to help. I have a notion for some reason that you may need all you can get.'

Which was a correct notion, as I shortly learned.

I went downstairs to the street, bright and hot with sunlight again after yesterday's rain, the heat more bothersome now than it had been before because the comfort index was way up close to the temperature, and I worked up a quick sweat walking three blocks to Hec Caldwell's office. It was his private office, a couple of rooms above a men's clothing store, and when I got there Hec was waiting for me behind his desk, and Cotton McBride was standing at a window with his back to the room and looking down into the street through the upper section of the window above a one-ton air conditioner installed in the lower.

Cotton's presence was all I needed to confirm my feeling that something was surely up, or rather out, and I had a pretty certain idea that what was out was my nocturnal idiocy in Dreamer's Park, but I couldn't for the life of me imagine how Cotton and Hec had learned about it.

Hec stood up and asked me to sit

down, which I did. Cotton turned away from the window and stood there looking at me with an expression that suggested a bad taste in his mouth, while Hec sat down again and started looking at me too, and between the pair of them, staring like that, they made me damn uncomfortable.

'Well,' I said, 'you asked me to come over right away, and here I am.'

'So you are,' Hec said. 'Thanks for coming.'

'What's the occasion?'

'No occasion. Just something that's come up. We hope you can help us with it.'

'Anything to oblige. What do you want me to do?'

'What we want you to do,' Cotton said, 'is quit playing fancy with me and everyone else and tell the truth for a change.'

'Who says I haven't been telling the truth, and who says what it is that I haven't been telling it about?'

'I say it, that's who says it, and what it's about is the murder of Beth Thatcher, and I'm the one who says that too. Anyhow, you haven't been telling *all* the truth, if any part of it, and you'd better start telling it right now if you know what's good for you.'

'I'm not so sure about that. I've just recently had advice from two pretty shrewd characters, and one of them presented a convincing case for the advantages of telling lies, and the other one said not to admit anything.'

'There's no need to get excited,' Hec said. 'Gid, Cotton's somewhat annoyed with you, as you can see, and maybe he's justified, and maybe he isn't. That's what we want to find out.'

'I'm all for that,' I said. 'Let's.'

'All right.' Hec opened the belly drawer of his desk and took out an envelope, which he held between a thumb and index finger. 'This was delivered to the police station this morning. Regular mail. You'd better read it.'

He passed it across the desk, and I took it. The envelope was perfectly dry, of course, but it gave me in my fingertips a sensation of unpleasant dampness. It was a cheap envelope, about 3½ by 6½, addressed with a typewriter. Pica type.

Local postmark. I removed a single sheet of paper from the envelope and read what was on it, and this was what:

To the police: *Ask Gideon Jones what he was doing in Dreamer's Park the night Beth Thatcher was killed. Don't let him tell you he wasn't there, because he was, and I saw him.* No signature, of course. No *X*'s and *O*'s for love and kisses. I put the sheet back into the envelope and handed it across the desk to Hec, who took it and dropped it on his blotter. I wiped my hands on the legs of my pants.

'I thought you said this was no occasion,' I said. 'I beg to differ. I've just been accused of murder for the first time in my life, and in my judgment that's an occasion as big as any there is.'

'Who accused you of murder?'

'Whoever wrote that note.'

'No. The note just said to ask you what you were doing in Dreamer's Park, and we're asking. What were you doing?'

'Assuming that I was there at all to be doing anything?'

'True. I'll put that question first. Were you there?'

Well, what the hell! Sid had told me to lie and had patiently explained the advantages of it, and I wanted to lie and had the lie all ready on my tongue, a single lousy little two-letter word beginning with *n* and ending with *o*, but I couldn't pronounce it.

It wasn't that I was shaken up or confused or anything like that, for I was thinking clearly and could see that the chances were good for lying and getting away with it, and the reason the chances were good, as I saw it, was because the writer of the note had not signed it. This meant that he or she did not wish to be identified and would probably never come forward to testify, and this was understandable when you stopped to consider all the implications, for in order to have seen me in Dreamer's Park, the writer, he or she, would have necessarily had to be in it too, or near it, and why should the police make any more of my having been there the night Beth was killed than of his or her having been there the same night? All I had to do was get a consonant and vowel off my tongue in proper order, but I couldn't do it, I simply couldn't, and so I told the truth and made an admission at the same time in spite of the sagest advice from separate sources to do neither.

'Yes,' I said.

Hec looked surprised and uncomfortable, and Cotton looked something I couldn't see, for I wasn't looking at him. I could hear him, though, and I heard him make a little wet smacking sound with his lips that seemed to have in it a quality of satisfaction.

'Do you know what you're saying?' Hec said.

'Certainly I know,' I said. 'I said I was in Dreamer's Park, and I was.'

'Why the hell didn't you say so before?' Cotton said.

'You didn't ask me,' I said.

'It's your God damn duty to tell something like that to the police without being asked,' Cotton said.

'That's right, Gid,' Hec said. 'You know it is. You should have told Cotton. Why didn't you?'

'That should be obvious,' I said. 'I

174

didn't tell because I wanted to avoid exactly what I haven't. I wanted to avoid being suspected of killing someone I didn't.'

'I don't know that you're suspected of killing anyone yet,' Hec said.

'As for me,' Cotton said, 'I don't know that he isn't.'

'That's what I thought,' I said.

'You'd better tell us why you went there and what you did there,' Hec said.

'I'll be happy to,' I said. 'I went there to meet Beth at her request, but I didn't meet her because she was dead.'

'Why the hell didn't you report her death to the police?' Cotton said. 'Don't you know there's a law about reporting bodies when you find them?'

'I didn't report it because I didn't know it.'

'God damn it, you just said she was dead. Now you say you didn't know it.'

'Oh, come off, Cotton. Why don't you quit trying to be a detective every minute? I said she was dead because she was later found dead. Putting that fact with the fact that she failed to meet me after arranging the meeting herself, I merely assumed that the failure was the result of her being dead.'

'You mean to say she might have been dead in that old bandstand all the time you were there and you didn't even see her?'

I considered my answer carefully for a split second, and I decided that the truth was fine as far as it went, but it was possible to try to make it go too far. Having reached this decision, I retreated to Sid's prepared position.

'I mean to say,' I said.

'What I can't figure out,' Hec said, 'is why you agreed to meet her in Dreamer's Park in the middle of the night, of all places and all times. There doesn't seem to me to be any good reason for it.'

'As for me,' Cotton said, 'I can think of *two* good reasons, and the other one's murder.'

'You aren't even half right,' I said. 'Dreamer's Park is a place of sentiment, and we were going to say a proper goodbye, and it seemed appropriate to say it in a sentimental place. Besides, I had been listening to cicadas and drinking gin.'

'It's a fact, Cotton, that Dreamer's Park is a place of sentiment,' Hec said. 'In my time, I've made a few connections there myself.'

'Well,' Cotton said, 'nooky is one thing, and murder's another, and I don't think we ought to be mixing them up in our thinking.'

'Cotton's right, Gid,' Hec said. 'We've got to keep sentiment out of this. Maybe you'd better just tell us what happened in your own words.'

'To begin with,' I said, 'I was pretty restless, the evening coming on for what it was plainly going to be, and then I met Beth after a lot of years in the Kiowa Room.'

'We know all about that,' Cotton said.

'Yes, Gid,' Hec said, 'just skip along to a little later. Tell us how it happened that you agreed to meet her.'

'It wouldn't have happened at all,' I said, 'if Sid hadn't gone off to talk with Rose Pogue about Zoroaster.'

'About who?' Cotton said.

'About whom?' Hec said.

'Never mind,' I said. 'Who or whom, off she went to talk, and I was alone in the house drinking gimlets and listening to 'Death and Transfiguration.' Then the phone rang, and it was Beth. She said she was going away the next day, and would I come to meet her and say goodbye, and I asked where. That was when she thought of Dreamer's Park, and it seemed like a fine place to say goodbye, with sentimental connections and all, and I agreed to go there to meet her.'

'What time was this?' Cotton said. He had a little notebook out, and was taking notes.

'I'm not sure,' I said. 'As I explained, I'd been drinking gimlets. I'm pretty sure it was pretty late, though. About nine-thirty.'

'Go on, Gid,' Hec said.

'There isn't much farther to go. Just across town to Dreamer's Park. When I got there, I sat in the bandstand and waited for Beth, but she didn't come, and finally I decided that she had simply found someone else to do something more interesting with. I went home and went to bed, and the next day I heard she'd been murdered, and that's all there is to it.'

'I've got a feeling,' Cotton said, 'that there may be more.'

'Did you see anyone at all while you were in the park?' Hec said.

'No one,' I said, 'except a few people at a distance passing along the streets. No one in the park itself.'

'What I was wondering specifically,' Hec said, 'is whether you saw anyone who might have seen you who might have written this note.'

'I didn't,' I said.

'That's too bad. I don't care too much for anonymous notes, if you want to know the truth. You got any enemies who might want to get you involved in a murder out of pure meanness?'

'None that I know of.'

'You'd better think hard. Someone you put in jail or something?'

'I've never put anyone in jail. My talents have been employed in trying to keep everyone out. I've sued a few for modest amounts, but never for enough to justify this kind of retaliation. In fact, the only person I've offended recently is Mrs. Roscoe Burdock, and I'm reasonably certain that she can't write, even on a typewriter.'

'I agree that Mrs. Burdock doesn't seem likely. I must say, Gid, that you aren't helping yourself much.'

'As for me,' Cotton said, 'I don't see why we have to assume any God damn enemy at all. I don't see why we can't assume a good citizen who is against murder and wanted to tell the police something they should have been told sooner by someone else.'

'I'm strongly in favor of good citizens myself,' I said. 'I'm almost as strongly for them as I am against being accused anonymously of murder.'

'Hold on, Gid,' Hec said. 'You weren't accused anonymously of murder. I pointed that out before. You were only accused of being where a murder was committed about the time it was.'

'That's a great satisfaction,' I said. 'Thanks for pointing it out.'

'However,' Hec said, 'we still have the problem of what to do with you.'

'That's no problem,' Cotton said.

'What's your suggestion?' Hec said.

'What we have to do,' Cotton said, 'is hold him on suspicion.'

'I guess that's right,' Hec said. 'I'm sorry, Gid, but I guess we have to hold you. You see how it is? You were there and all, and you didn't tell about it, and that makes you suspicious at the very least.'

'Thanks again,' I said. 'I feel chosen. May I go back to my office and tidy things up a bit?'

'I'm against it,' Cotton said. 'You can't let a murder suspect run around loose to do things like that.'

'By God, Cotton,' I said, 'it's impossible for me to tell you how much I admire your devotion to duty. Do you think it would be permissible to make a couple of telephone calls?'

'I can't see any harm in a couple of telephone calls,' Hec said. 'Can you, Cotton?'

'That depends on who he calls and what he says,' Cotton said.

'Who are you going to call, Gid?' Hec said.

'A couple of pretty seamy characters, if you must know. Millie Morgan at the office for one, and Sid Jones at home for another.'

'What are you going to say?' Cotton said.

'That may turn out to be a problem, now that you've put it to me. Not so much with Millie, maybe. After all, she's only my secretary, and I guess I'll just tell her directly that I'm going to jail for an indeterminate period, and ask her to sort of sit on things at the office for the duration if she can bear the association with a homicidal idiot. Sid's another matter, however. As a wife, she may be expected to react a little more aggressively to the news that her husband is under arrest on suspicion of murder, and she may require a delicate approach. Can anyone suggest how I could tell my wife delicately that I'm going to jail?'

'I don't have any suggestions,' Hec said. 'Do you, Cotton?'

'How the hell would I know?' Cotton

said. 'I don't even have a wife.'

'Gid,' Hec said, 'I guess you'll just have to go ahead and call and do the best you can.'

'Thanks. May I use your phone?'

'Sure. Go ahead and use it.'

I did, dialing the office number first, and Millie answered.

'Hello, Millie,' I said.

'Is that you, Gid? Where the hell are you?'

'I'm in the office of Hector Caldwell, attorney-at-law.'

'Why are you calling? Why don't you come back and tell me what he wanted with you?'

'Unfortunately, that's not possible at this time.'

'Will you be long? I can hardly wait to hear.'

'Well, don't hold your hand on your tail while you're waiting, honey, because it might grow there.'

'Damn it, Gid, I simply can't understand you. What do you mean, my hand might grow to my tail? What a hell of a thing to say!'

'Sorry, honey. More whistling. What I mean is, it appears at the moment that my absence may be prolonged. Cotton McBride, who is listening to this end of our conversation, is of the opinion that it may be permanent. In brief, I've been hauled into custody.'

'Are you serious?'

'Never more so.'

'Didn't I warn you about that son of a bitch Hector Caldwell? And Cotton McBride is worse, if possible. Have you admitted anything? What are you suspected of?'

'I'm suspected of murdering Beth Thatcher.'

'The hell you are! You didn't, did you?'

'I'm happy to say I didn't.'

'I didn't think you did, really.'

'It's too bad that present company isn't as easily convinced.'

'Cotton and Hector? Those two bastards have absolutely no brain between them.'

'I'm inclined to agree, but it's beside the point. The point is, I'm under arrest, and I'll be detained a while, and I wonder if you'll sit on things at the office and more or less keep me in practice until further notice?'

'I've got some things here right now that need your signature. Do you want me to forge it?'

'You'd better not. One of us in jail at a time is more than enough. After I'm settled in my new accommodations, I'll be allowed short visits from friends and associates, I think. Bring the papers over tomorrow, and I'll sign them.'

'I'll be there. And don't you worry, Gid. I'll bet you're out of that jail in no time. Is there anything I can do to help? Maybe I could get that Hec Caldwell in a compromising position that would enable us to put some pressure on him.'

'Don't bother, please. Just be a good girl and take care of things. Goodbye, now.'

I hung up and took a deep breath, getting ready for Sid, and began to dial my residence number. Hec Caldwell leaned back in his swivel chair and looked past me at Cotton McBride with an expression of complacency.

'You see, Cotton?' he said. 'Nothing at all was said that could do the least harm.'

'Nothing harmful was said at this end of the line,' Cotton said, 'but I'm not so sure about the other.'

'What harmful could she have possibly said? You tend, as a policeman, to be excessively suspicious, Cotton.'

'That's a smart-aleck redhead, in case you don't know it, and it comes natural to her to say harmful things.'

'As a matter of fact,' I said, 'our conversation was innocent at both ends. The only thing about it that you might find objectionable was her calling you a pair of sons of bitches and bastards.'

'There you are,' Cotton said. 'That's a smart-aleck redhead if I ever saw one. She has no respect for any one.'

'Why did she want to call us names like that?' Hec said. 'That's no way to talk about public officials.'

'She was a little upset because you arrested me,' I said. 'She's slightly prejudiced in my favor.'

'I can appreciate her being upset and prejudiced,' Hec said, 'but I still don't like

186

being called a son of a bitch and a bastard. Either one is bad enough, and both at once are just too damn much.'

I had dialed, and the phone was ringing. It rang and rang and no one answered. I was just about to hang up, having decided that Sid had gone out somewhere, when all of a sudden she was on the line breathlessly.

'Hello, hello,' she said. 'Who's there?'

'I'm here,' I said.

'Gid?'

'Gid the mate of Sid. Sid and Gid Jones, that is.'

'Sugar, I was out on the back terrace taking a sun bath, and after a while I barely heard the phone ringing after I don't know how long, and I ran in as fast as I could to answer. I'm so glad I got here before you hung up.'

'Are you wearing your white bathing suit?'

'Yes, I am. I always wear the white one when I'm sun bathing, because it leaves the most of me out in the sun.'

'I've observed that before, and I wish I was there to observe it now.'

'So do I, sugar. I'd much rather be observed by you than that Jack Handy next door. He's been out in his backyard all morning, and half the time he's been peering at me through the hedge. He's a regular God damn peeping Tom.'

'At least he's a discriminating peeping Tom. You ought to feel flattered. If one must be addicted to voyeurism, it's in his favor to be selective.'

'Voyeurism? What's that?'

'That's peeping.'

'Oh. Is that what it is? Sugar, is everything all right? Why did you call?'

'I called to tell you that I won't be home for dinner tonight.'

'How exasperating! Why won't you? Where will you be for dinner?'

'For dinner I'll be in the county jail as the guest of Cotton McBride and Hector Caldwell.'

'Don't be ridiculous. No one has dinner in the county jail.'

'Oh, yes, someone does. A number do, as a matter of fact. The prisoners, I mean.'

'What's that? Prisoners? Are you sure you're sober? I hope for your sake, as well as mine, that this isn't the beginning of another gimlet affair.'

'No. Not at all. Whatever they serve in the county jail, I'm sure they don't serve gimlets.'

'Sugar, you sound rather confused. I can't quite make any sense of what you're saying. Are you trying to tell me something that you don't quite have the courage to tell me directly?'

'I guess that's it.'

'Tell me what it is at once. Do you hear me?'

'I hear you. What I'm trying to tell you is that I'm being arrested on suspicion of the murder of Beth Thatcher, and as a consequence I'm being taken into custody, which is a way of saying that I'm being put into jail.'

'Nonsense. How can you be arrested for killing someone you didn't kill? Who's arresting you? Is it that God damn Cotton McBride?'

'Cotton and Hec. It's a cooperative job.'

'Where is that McBride? Is he there?'

'Right here. Old rabbit ears himself.'

'Put him on the phone. I want to talk to him immediately.'

'I don't think I want to. He's already sufficiently annoyed with me.'

'What I'd like to know is how the hell they can arrest you without any reason whatever.'

'They think they have one. Someone wrote a note and told them that I went to Dreamer's Park the night Beth was killed.'

'Here, now, by God!' Cotton said. 'You can't talk to her about that.'

'Cotton's right, Gid,' Hec said. 'You can't talk about the evidence.'

'Go to hell,' I said.

'What did you say?' Sid said. 'Did you tell me to go to hell?'

'Not you. Cotton and Hec.'

'Oh. That's all right, then. That's nothing to what I'll tell them the first chance I get. Who wrote the note?'

'I don't know. It wasn't signed.'

'Well, an unsigned note doesn't prove anything. Any nut could write an unsigned note. Surely, after what I told you, you denied being there.'

'I didn't, unfortunately. I admitted it.'

'Admitted it? Actually? Sugar, were you temporarily insane or something? I told you explicitly to say that you were at home all night.'

'I know you did, and I tried, but somehow or other I just couldn't do it.'

'Why not? What was to prevent you?'

'Hell, I can't explain it. It may have been a supernatural influence.'

'Sugar, you mustn't begin to imagine things. It's the worst kind of sign. The damage has been done now, and we'll simply have to make the best of it. It's perfectly clear to me that I must take a hand in this directly if anything sensible is ever to be done.'

'What do you plan to do?'

'I don't know at this moment, but I'll think of something.'

She was silent for a few seconds, as if she had already begun to think, and when she spoke again her voice had receded and saddened. 'I'll have to think of something all the time to avoid thinking of you in jail. Sugar, I can't bear to think of you in jail.'

'I can hardly bear it myself.'

'I'll come down to see you as soon as possible and bring you a few things that you may need.'

'Sid, I'm sorry.'

'For what, sugar?'

'For everything.'

'Oh, no. Not for everything. There are a few things that have happened recently that you may be sorry about if it does you any good, but in most ways most of the time you have nothing to be sorry about at all. You've been a superior and interesting husband, all in all, and I love you as much as ever and maybe more.'

'And I you and no maybe. More and more and more.'

'Sugar, I'm about to cry, and I don't want to.'

'I've got to hang up now. Will you be all right out there in Hoolihan's Addition all alone?'

'I don't intend to be alone very long. I promise that you'll be back almost before you know you've been gone. You just wait and see.'

'Apparently I'll have to.'

'And you tell that bastard McBride not to come sneaking around here picking my brains again if he doesn't want to be shot as a trespasser. I'll tell him myself if you'll only put him on the phone.'

'I'll tell him. Goodbye, Sid.'

'Goodbye, sugar.'

That was about it. I put the phone in its cradle and pushed it away from me. It had been bad enough, as it had to be, but not as bad as it might have been.

'Tell who what?' Cotton said.

'You're who,' I said, 'and what is that you'd better not come sneaking around picking Sid's brains again if you don't want to be shot.'

'What the hell's the matter with that woman? She can't be threatening an officer of the law in line of duty.'

'She also called you a bastard. That makes two people in ten minutes. I'm beginning to think there must be some truth in it.'

'She wasn't responsible,' Hec said. 'You've got to realize, Cotton, that it puts a strain on a wife to learn that her husband's going to jail. Did she say anything about me, Gid?'

'Nothing much. She concentrated on Cotton.'

'Well, I suppose she'll never speak to me again after this.' He stood up behind his desk and looked strong and resigned and slightly noble. 'It's one of the penalties of a job like mine. You do your plain duty, no matter how much it may hurt you inside, and someone always hates you for it.'

'As I see it,' Cotton said, 'my plain duty right now is to take the prisoner over to the county jail, and I'm going to do it.'

'That's right, Gid,' Hec said. 'It's Cotton's duty to do it.'

So he did his duty, and we went. I had tried to be brave and assured and all that prideful stuff, and maybe I managed to make the picture pretty well, but I didn't feel it. Inside, like Hec, I was hurting.

I have a notion I was hurting worse.

11

The county jail was located in the oldest residential area of town, a red brick building erected near the turn of the century in the center of a square block of grass and trees and flowering shrubs. A brick walk led up to the building from the street, a pattern of moss in the cracks between bricks, and the walls of the building were covered with ivy. It had not changed in appearance in my time, and I suppose it had not changed appreciably in fifty years or more, except to age and mellow and acquire as the years passed a soft deceptive air of being something better than it was.

Inside, the floors were darkened by innumerable applications of varnish and sweeping compound, and the air was heavy with the scent of cedar.

Entering, I had for a moment the captured feeling of being a kid again in another time, say ten or twelve a quarter of a century back, and I was coming into school on my way to the room for grade four or six.

The building was two stories high, and my accommodations were second floor rear, northeast corner. There was a narrow barred window in the east wall and another narrow barred window in the north wall, and thus I had the luxury of double exposure, which was something, I learned, that no other cell in the whole place had, and I think this was in deference to my status as a murder suspect among petty offenders.

There was a bunk for sleeping attached to a wall. There was a lavatory for washing. There was a commode.

In the middle of the afternoon of that first day, I was standing at the north window looking sometimes down through bars into the side yard where the dark grass was patterned by shade and sun, and sometimes out levelly into leaves of oaks and maples and sycamores. It was an old and quiet and beautiful yard in which kids might have played for hours on summer days, much too nice a yard for a jail to have, and there were, in fact, two kids playing there at this time, two boys in jeans.

They were sitting cross-legged on the grass, facing each other and deeply intent upon what was happening between them, and what was happening, I saw, was a game of mumblety-peg. One of the boys would take the pocket knife and go through as many of the tricks as he could without missing, and then the other boy in his turn would do likewise, and I began to try to remember as many of the tricks as I could of the game as I used to play it. I found that I could remember most of the tricks, how they were done, but only three of the names for them, and the three names I remembered were Dropping the Devil through the Well, Spanking Baby's Bottom, and Jumping the Pasture Fence. This was one way to keep from thinking of Sid and the trouble I was causing her through idiocy, but not a very good one or a very successful one, and I kept thinking of her in spite of boys in jeans and mumblety-peg.

I had been in jail four hours, but they

seemed like four weeks, and the four had become five when Harley Murchison, the jailer, came up and opened my grill and said that I had a visitor.

He took me down to a small room on the first floor, and there was Sid. The walls and floor of the room were bare, and there was a long table in the middle of the room with three straight chairs along each side. Overhead, slowly revolving, was an old-fashioned ceiling fan that slapped and stirred the hot air into sluggish motion.

Sid was standing with her back to a north window, and out in the yard beyond her were the pair of kids in jeans playing mumblety-peg. She was wearing a white sleeveless dress and white ballerina slippers, and she looked brown and sad and somehow younger than she had ever looked to me before. I went over and put my arms around her, and she hung on for a few seconds, and I could hear a little choking sound in her throat, followed by a sniff in her nose.

'God damn son of a bitch,' she said.

'Who?' I said.

'Nobody. It's just an old trick. When I want to cry, I curse instead, and it's very effective. The stronger the cursing, the more effective it is.'

'I'll have to remember that. I may be able to use it.'

I sat down in a chair by the table, and she sat down in one beside me. We held hands.

'What have you been doing?' I said.

'I've been trying to run down that bastard Cotton McBride, that's what I've been doing, but he's never anywhere I go, or at least someone says he isn't, and it's perfectly apparent by this time that he's trying to avoid me.'

'Perhaps it's just as well.'

'Do you think so? Well, I don't, not by a damn sight, and he surely can't avoid me forever, no matter how much he may want to.'

'Have you talked with anyone at all?'

'Only Hector Caldwell. I went to his office after I had temporarily given up finding Cotton McBride. He was so damn full of noble regrets and windy pretensions that I was nearly sick on his carpet, but at least he called here to the jail and said that I was to be allowed to see you and was to be shown every courtesy and consideration, all that, and so here I am, and I have a few things for you in this sack.'

'Thanks very much for bringing them.'

'They're just a few little things, sugar. A safety razor and some soap and a few paperbacks. Just a few things like that. Harley Murchison looked at them and said it was all right for you to have them.'

'Thanks most of all for bringing yourself.'

'You mustn't thank me for that. It implies that I have done something out of kindness, which isn't true. It's only natural, since I love you, for me to come wherever you may be.'

'If you love me, will you do something for me?'

'I'm not sure. Possibly I'll *refuse* to do it because I love you. I'm forced to recognize that you're not always the best judge of what is for your own good. However, what do you want me to do?'

'I want you to go home and be good.

Let me get out of this the best I can alone.'

'Excuse me, sugar, but I have no confidence whatever that you could get out of it at all without my help.'

'I'll get out of it, all right. It's merely a matter of a little time.'

'I simply can't understand what gives you such assurance. To this point, in spite of my telling you exactly what to do and say in certain situations, you have shown almost no ability for getting out of it. On the contrary, you keep getting deeper and deeper *into* it. Please tell me why you think things will be any different hereafter.'

'Because this anonymous note isn't sufficient evidence to base an indictment on, and Hec Caldwell knows it. My arrest on suspicion is just a kind of gesture, that's all. Maybe Hec and Cotton think they can get more evidence that will support a charge, but they can't because there isn't any. Pretty soon, they'll have to let me go.'

'There. That's exactly what I mean. What you have just said only confirms my conviction of how irresponsible and reckless you are. It makes my blood run cold to hear you talk. First you exaggerate your own ability to handle matters, which is not supported by events, and now you assume without any earthly reason that Hec Caldwell will suddenly begin to think and behave intelligently. This is clearly impossible, for he doesn't have the necessary brains, and he is, moreover, under the influence of Cotton McBride in this case, who has even less. No, no, sugar, I'll not stay out of it, and what I want you to do now, without any further delay, is tell me exactly what was said in the telephone conversation between you and Beth while I was away talking about Zoroaster with Rose Pogue.'

'I've already told you what was said.'

'Only generally, however. Not exactly.'

'I can't remember exactly. As I've reported, I'd been drinking gimlets, and my mind wasn't as sharp as usual.'

'You can remember if you try. It's well known that almost anything can be remembered, even from early childhood, if one makes proper associations and really concentrates.'

'It sounds like hard work. Why do you want to know what was said exactly?'

'You never know, sugar. Maybe something significant was said to which, because of gin or dullness, you didn't attach sufficient importance.'

'I don't think so, but I'll associate and concentrate if you insist.'

'I do insist. It wasn't long ago, actually, and shouldn't be extremely difficult.'

'Well, there I was in the living room. You had gone off in your pale yellow dress to Rose Pogue's, and I was feeling lonely and scorned. I was drinking a gimlet and wanted to listen to some music, and I considered Haydn, as always, but I decided against him because he seemed a little too damn gay for the occasion, and then I found 'Death and Transfiguration,' by Richard Strauss, and that's what I played. It was still playing when the phone rang in the hall, and I went out and answered it, and it was Beth, as you know, and that's when the conversation started.'

'Good. You're doing marvelously, sugar.

Just begin at the beginning of the conversation, and don't leave anything out for the sake of discretion. What you might leave out could be the most significant of everything, and we can settle later any issue that may arise from your being honest.'

'All right. First, she asked if it was me on the phone, and I said it was. Then she asked me what I was doing, and I said I was drinking gimlets and listening to 'Death and Transfiguration,' and she said something about drinking gimlets still, and I said not still, but again, because I had taken time out for a bottle of white Burgundy. What was said after that for a while is pretty hazy, but I'm fairly sure it concerned the music, which she could hear, and the state of my emotions, which was gloomy.

'Then she asked if you were home, and I said no, that you were off discussing Zoroaster with Rose Pogue, and she said that something like that with Rose might go on forever. Right after that she asked me if I would meet her somewhere, and I asked where, and she remembered Dreamer's Park and suggested it, and I agreed to go. And that's all of what was said that I can remember, as exactly as I remember it.'

'That clears up what was said, then. Is there anything you want to add or change regarding what was *done*?'

'Oh, no. Absolutely not. I told you what happened as it really did, but I ought to warn you that I didn't tell quite all the truth to Hec and Cotton. What I didn't tell them was that I found the body and didn't report it.'

'It's a relief to learn that you followed my instructions to that extent, at least. It would be too bad to have you kept in jail for such a minor offense after you have been proved innocent of a major one.'

'Yes, it would. I couldn't agree with you more.'

'Are you positive you've told me all you can remember of what was said?'

'All. Did I say anything significant that I failed to understand because of gin or dullness?'

'That remains to be seen. I admit that nothing significant is apparent, but perhaps I'll discover something if I keep thinking about it.'

About that time Harley Murchison came to the door and coughed, which was a sign that it was time for Sid to go. I stood up, and so did Sid, and Harley went away again to give us a chance to say a private goodbye in our own way, and I took advantage of the chance. I held her and kissed her and took a deep breath of the scent of her hair to smell after she was gone, and she said, 'God damn son of a bitch,' as she had before, in order to keep from crying.

'You're not a bad sort,' I said. 'As wives go, you're quite satisfactory.'

'I know, sugar. In some ways, I'm even exceptional.'

'I'm very glad that you've come to see me, and I hope you'll come again. Now, however, since you must go, I'd appreciate it if you would go quickly. I don't want to humiliate myself by an unmanly exhibition. I have a certain status here that I must maintain. After all, I'm the only prisoner suspected of killing someone, and I'm rather looked up to. Harley and I are going to play dominoes this evening. He's already asked me, and I've accepted.'

She sniffed and wiped her nose and went, and where she went and what she did, while I went nowhere and did nothing, make a story that you may not believe if I haven't been able to make you see her as she was. I don't know exactly what she did and said in all instances, for I wasn't with her, but I'm sure I can use my imagination and tell it all with verisimilitude, if not with precise accuracy, from what she told me afterward, and what I heard from others, and most of all from simply knowing Sid and what, in given circumstances, she would most likely do and say.

Where she went first, after leaving the county jail and me in it, was to my office to see Millie Morgan. It was getting pretty late in the afternoon by that time, and Millie was getting ready to close up and go home when Sid arrived. As a matter of probability, she was sitting sidewise to her desk with her legs crossed and a mirror in one hand and a lipstick in the other. I'm willing to commit myself to this because repairing her lips was almost always Millie's last activity before leaving, and what the crossed legs contributed to it I don't know, but they seemed to be essential.

'Here you still are, Millie,' Sid said. 'I was afraid you might be gone.'

'A few minutes later I'd have been,' Millie said, 'but I'm glad I'm not. Have you seen Gid since that God damn Hec Caldwell put him in jail?'

'I just came from seeing him. I don't think it was so much Hec who put him there, however, as Cotton McBride.'

'In my opinion, they were both in it and equally responsible. Anyhow, Hec is the county attorney and is expected to act as if he had some intelligence. Cotton is more easily excused because no one could reasonably expect anything of him that required a brain. What on earth makes them suspect Gid of having murdered Beth Thatcher? He called me on the phone and said they did, but he didn't say why, and I've been dying to know ever since.'

'Because he went to Dreamer's Park

the night she was killed there, and someone apparently saw him and wrote a note to the police about it.'

'Well, what a damn dirty trick! To write such a note, I mean, and deliberately get someone into all this trouble. Whoever did it?'

'That's not known, for the note wasn't signed.'

'Isn't it rather odd that Gid would go to Dreamer's Park in the middle of the night? Did you know he was going?'

'No. I only learned that he went after he had gone. I was away from home at the time, talking with Rose Pogue.'

'You don't seem much disturbed by it all, except that it's got him in jail, and so I assume that his reason for going there, whatever it was, was innocent enough.'

'I'm not quite convinced that his reason for going was so damn innocent, I must admit, but it came to nothing, as it turned out, which makes it much easier to forgive him. To tell the truth, he went there to meet Beth Thatcher.'

'The hell he did! If he were my husband, I don't believe I'd be quite so amiable about something like that as you seem to be.'

'It's not that I'm so amiable, really. It's only that I'm forced by circumstances to appear so. I may yet, when the time is right, decide to deprive him temporarily of a few privileges for going off like that the minute my back was turned. Now, however, he is in jail and in trouble, and I must do what I can to get him out. It's perfectly clear that this is far too serious to be left in the hands of incompetents like Hec Caldwell and Cotton McBride. Whatever Gid may have intended to do in Dreamer's Park and didn't, I don't wish to have him hanged or taken away from me permanently as a consequence.'

'I agree with you there. It would be unfortunate to have anything very grim happen to him, although a little discomfort and a temporary loss of privileges seem to be in order. What do you intend to do?'

'I'm not sure. I'll have to investigate the situation and see what I can discover. As a beginning, I've been trying to find that sneaky bastard McBride, but he's been avoiding me.'

'That's a good sign, if you ask me. It shows how uncertain of himself he is. What do you expect to do to him when you catch him?'

'I expect to ask him some questions, that's what.'

'Is that all? I was in hopes it would be more.'

'I can hardly afford to assault a policeman, no matter how offensive he is or how much he may deserve it. There's very little I could do to clear this matter up if I were in jail also.'

'That's true. You'll have to control your natural impulses if you wish to remain free to operate. Is there anything in particular that I can do to help?'

'Not immediately. There may be something later, however, and it's reassuring to know that you're available. I can't tell you how much I appreciate it.'

'Don't mention it. In the meanwhile, I'll keep things open and going here at the office, although I don't imagine there will be much to do after it becomes generally known that Gid is in jail. It's difficult, if not impossible, to practice law in a cell.'

'As a legal secretary, do you think his practice will suffer after his release? After all, people may be a little reluctant to employ a lawyer who has been suspected of murder, and worst of all, who behaved like a perfect simpleton in order to get himself suspected.'

'I wouldn't worry about it if I were you. It's my professional opinion that his practice will benefit, if anything. He will get a certain amount of publicity, which is always good in the end, and when he is proved innocent, thanks to you, everyone will eventually forget how it really was and think that it was due to his own cleverness as a lawyer.'

'That's quite encouraging, I must say. I respect your opinion, and I've always felt that you have a great deal more to do with the efficiency of this office than is generally conceded. Would you like to go somewhere and have a drink or something?'

'I'd like to, but I don't think I'd better. I'm scheduled for a skirmish with a certain engineer this evening, and I need to keep a clear head.'

'In that case, I'll run along. Goodbye for the present.'

'Goodbye,' Millie said. 'Let me know the instant I'm needed.'

Sid went downstairs and stood for a moment on the sidewalk to consider her immediate future. She thought at first that she would go home and apply herself to devising a plan of action of some kind, but then she thought that she might as well try once more to catch Cotton McBride, and so she went over to the police department in City Hall, and Cotton was there, and she caught him.

'Here you are at last,' Sid said. 'Where the devil have you been?'

Cotton was sitting at his desk, inserted to his hips in the kneehole, and he stood up so quickly and carelessly that he banged one knee against the under edge of his belly drawer, which was not only painful but also added to an effect of guilty confusion.

'I've been busy,' he said.

'That's certainly so. I won't argue with

that. You've been busy making mistakes and the worst kind of fool of yourself. Why have you put Gid in jail without a word of warning to me or anyone else?'

'I put him in jail because he's a murder suspect, that's why.'

'And why, precisely, do you consider him a murder suspect?'

'You know as well as I do why he's considered a suspect. Because he was seen in Dreamer's Park about the time Beth Thatcher was murdered there.'

'Are you sure? What time was that?'

'He said he left home about nine-thirty, and he walked to the park, so it must have been around ten o'clock.'

'Truly? That's very astute of you. It's incredible how you can make such clever deductions. I wasn't asking what time Gid was there, however, for I knew long before you did. I was asking what time Beth Thatcher was murdered.'

Cotton, who had his mouth open in position for his next remark, stood looking at her for a few seconds in silence, his mouth still open in position, and then he sat down slowly in his chair and took a firm grip on its arms. Sid, uninvited, sat down in a chair across from him.

'That's not exactly known, of course,' Cotton said.

'How interesting! What time, *in*exactly, would you say she was killed?'

'Damn it, it's impossible to do more than make a scientific estimate. The coroner says it was almost certainly sometime between seven and eleven.'

'It must be wonderful to be able to make things like scientific estimates, and I don't see how that coroner manages to do it. He isn't even a doctor, let alone a scientist.'

'The post-mortem was done by a doctor.'

'Oh, yes. Naturally. A general practitioner who would have trouble diagnosing rigor mortis itself, without regard for the time it started.'

'Now, I'll tell you something, Mrs. Jones. You're always going around making critical remarks about the police and the medical profession, and I want to warn you that you'd better stop. It's not right.'

'Isn't it? Without making an issue of the fact that you've slightly exaggerated my position, I'd like to point out that being critical of a doctor and a policeman and a coroner is not quite so serious a matter as putting someone in jail for the silliest of reasons.'

'By God, Gid was in the park during the estimated time of death. He's admitted that he was, and that's reason enough to hold him.'

'I believe you said the estimated time of death is four hours. Seven to eleven. How many other people were in the park in that time?'

'How the hell would I know? We didn't have the damn park under surveillance.'

'That's a very significant admission, don't you think? Thank you for making it.'

'I'm not making any admissions or anything else. I'm only saying what's what. The point is, Gid's the only one we *know* was in the park, and he went there specifically to meet the victim, and he had a reason to hold a grudge against her.'

'Is that so? I'm especially interested in

that statement. What reason to hold a grudge?'

'You know what reason. She played him a damn dirty trick once.'

'By marrying someone else? On the contrary, she did him a favor. If she hadn't married someone else, Gid would never have had the chance to marry me.'

'Well, it's not my place to argue the relative merits of two women.'

'That's correct. It isn't. I'm glad to know that you know what your place isn't, even if you don't always seem to know what it is.'

'I'll have to repeat, however, that he went to meet her in the middle of the night in Dreamer's Park, and it's only natural to assume that his reason, murder or something else, was not to play patty-cake or ring-around-the-rosie.'

'Possibly that's because, not being the type that women care for, your assumptions are distorted by wishful thinking. Do you often engage in fantasy?'

Cotton took an even firmer grip on the arms of his chair, his knuckles turning white, and breathed deeply several times.

It was plain that Sid had touched him where touching hurt.

'There's nothing to be gained from our sitting here taking turns telling what we don't like about each other,' he said finally.

'I agree,' Sid said. 'From my point of view, it would take far too long, and it would be much more profitable to discuss the murder case. It's apparent, if you'll excuse my saying so, that it's high time it was investigated carefully by someone sensible. We have already established, for example, that you don't really know when the victim died or who was with her when she did. Now I would like to know what makes you so sure you know *where* she died.'

'Damn it, she died in Dreamer's Park.'

'How do you know? Did someone actually see her killed there?'

'No, but that's where she was found, and it's logical to assume that that's where she was killed.'

'Why?'

'Because no one in his right mind would be lugging a dead body around this town when it would be safer and easier to leave it where it became dead. Besides, Beth Thatcher called Gid and arranged to meet him in the park, and by God that's where she went and where she was killed.'

'It must be a great comfort to have a dogmatic mind. As for me, I'm never so sure about things. It occurs to me, although I've read about the murder in the newspaper and heard it talked about by various people, including you, that no one has ever made much of a point about blood. Was the weapon that killed her left in the wound?'

'It was not. We haven't found it yet, but we're looking for it, and we probably will. It'll be necessary, by the way, to search your house and yard.'

'We can settle that when the time comes. What I want to know now is how much blood there was.'

'Not much. Very little. The wound was just a sort of puncture, made by a thin blade.'

'It was deep, however, for it killed her. Wouldn't a deep wound like that bleed considerably, even a sort of puncture, when the weapon was pulled out?'

'The doc said most of the bleeding was internal.'

'Nevertheless, I consider it odd and interesting that more of it wasn't external. I'm convinced that a long blade, however thin, would cause considerable bleeding.'

'The doc says it wasn't exactly a blade, from the looks of the wound. It was more spike-like.'

'But the paper and everyone have kept saying blade.'

'It was just something that got said and repeated. As far as the public is concerned, what's the difference?'

'I'm not the public. I claim to be a participant, having Gid in jail, and I'm of the opinion that there's quite a difference between a blade and something spike-like. It's obvious that you've been either sloppy or deceptive in numerous instances. I'm willing to concede, however, that something spike-like would probably cause less bleeding than a blade.'

'Thanks so much.'

'But I reserve the right to think that

there *might* have been more bleeding elsewhere.'

'There wasn't. There wasn't an elsewhere, and there wasn't any more bleeding. As a matter of fact, there wasn't even enough bleeding to wash away all the dirt.'

'Dirt? Did you say dirt?'

'That's what I said. There must have been some dirt on the weapon, because there was some at the edge of the wound, and a little inside.'

'Well, this is getting more odd and interesting all the time, and it seems to me that you've given far too little attention to details that deserve more.' Sid stood up and smoothed her skirt over her hips, leaving her hands on them afterward as she looked down at Cotton. 'I gave you a significant lead only last Saturday, for instance, when you were at our house drinking one of our beers. Have you done the least thing about it?'

'It doesn't appear now that it will be necessary.'

'It may not appear necessary to you, but it does to me.'

'I'd better warn you not to interfere with police business.'

'Anything I do will not be interference. It will only be what you should have done yourself and didn't.' She turned and walked away a couple of steps and looked back over her shoulder. 'By the way,' she said, 'if you actually plan to waste time searching our yard and house, be sure you bring a warrant with you when you come to do it.'

'I know,' Cotton said sourly.

'Otherwise, you'll shoot me as a trespasser.'

12

The next morning Sid got up early and dressed and made coffee. While she was drinking the coffee alone at the kitchen table, she began to plan what she would do that day, and what she planned to do, first of all, was to go out to the Thatcher home and talk with Mrs. Thatcher.

She thought in the beginning that she would call and make an appointment, but then she reconsidered and thought that it might be better and more effective just to go on out. She had no reason to believe that she would be particularly welcome at any time, and even less so under existing conditions, and she did not wish to be told on the phone by a maid or someone that Mrs. Thatcher had a sick headache or had suddenly left town or anything like that. She was certain, however, that Mrs. Thatcher would not be an early riser, and that nine o'clock, or possibly ten, would be about the right time to go.

It was only seven-thirty when she was thinking this, and so she would have to do something else for a couple of hours, to compromise between nine and ten, before leaving.

She went out into the living room where she had left yesterday's edition of the local newspaper after reading it last night. She took the paper back to the kitchen and poured another cup of coffee and began to read again on the front page, continued on page three, the startling account of how Gideon Jones, prominent young local attorney, had been detained by authorities on suspicion of murdering Beth Webb Thatcher, formerly the wife of Wilson Thatcher, prominent young business executive.

She read the account carefully from beginning to end, as she had already done once before, and although the grounds for suspecting Gideon Jones were made perfectly clear in short words that could be understood even on the fringes of literacy, there was not the slightest suggestion that Mr. and Mrs. Wilson Thatcher were legally Wilson

Thatcher and Thelma Bleeker, unwed and unchaste, or that they had been blackmailed as a result by the legal Mrs. Wilson Thatcher, who was dead from having been killed, and might, therefore, quite reasonably be considered suspicious themselves.

Sid felt that this was discriminatory and unfair, and she suspected the connivance of Cotton McBride and Hec Caldwell.

There was clearly, at any rate, a minor conspiracy to spare the Thatchers public embarrassment unless it became absolutely unavoidable, and it was Sid's opinion, hotly held in indignation, that the Thatchers were not a damn bit more worthy of being spared than the Gideon Joneses, who had not been spared at all. There was even a bad picture of the suspect, me, and a more than slightly sexy one of the victim, Beth, and it was a safe bet that nine out of ten people who saw the latter came immediately to the conclusion that the subject of the former had been up to something considerably more interesting and entertaining than murder before murder was committed.

After a couple of tedious hours, about nine-thirty, Sid went on out to the Thatcher home. It was a big, high house on an old street, and it sat well back from the street behind a deep yard. There was an iron picket fence around the yard with a pair of stone deer inside it. A driveway approached the house in a flat curve from the street, running under a side portico and on to garages in the rear. The house was built, I think, in the early twenties, but it had about it an ugly Victorian air of pretentious elegance. There was not actually any ginger bread on it, but it looked as if there should have been.

Sid parked in the portico and went up side steps onto a high porch. She pushed a bell button beside a heavy door flanked by narrow panes of leaded glass, and pretty soon, as she had anticipated, the door was opened by a maid, who asked her what she wanted.

'I want to see Mrs. Wilson Thatcher,' Sid said. 'Please tell her that Mrs. Gideon Jones is calling.'

The name produced an effect that it

would not have produced before yesterday's newspaper, and the maid, after a quick recovery from a startled expression inappropriate to a proper maid, said that she would see if Mrs. Thatcher was in. Sid was allowed to wait in the hall while this was being done, and the waiting ran into several minutes, at least four or five, before the maid returned with Mrs. Thatcher's regrets that she was feeling indisposed and unable to receive anyone.

'In that case,' Sid said, 'I would like to see Miss Thelma Bleeker.'

'Who?' the maid said.

'Miss Thelma Bleeker.'

'I'm sorry. There's no one here with that name.'

'Nevertheless, I'd appreciate it if you would go and tell Mrs. Thatcher that Mrs. Gideon Jones wishes to speak with Miss Thelma Bleeker, and I don't mind telling you that it will be in her best interests if you do as I say.'

'If you will just wait here,' the maid said.

'I'll wait,' Sid said, 'but I don't care to wait quite as long as I did before. Try to be a little quicker, if you please.'

The maid went away again and came back again, this time quicker. Mrs. Thatcher, she said, had decided to see Mrs. Jones after all, and so Mrs. Jones followed the maid into a small room off the hall, where she was left, and pretty soon Mrs. Thatcher came to join her there, and with Mrs. Thatcher, somewhat to Mrs. Jones's surprise, was no one but Mr. Thatcher.

'Good morning, Mrs. Jones,' Wilson Thatcher said. 'It's a pleasure to see you again.'

'As a matter of fact,' Sid said, 'it clearly isn't, and we will probably all feel more comfortable if no one tries to pretend that it is.'

'Well, it's a difficult time for you, I know, and I would like you to believe, at least, that you have our sympathy.'

'So far as that goes, the time is not nearly so difficult for me as some later time is going to be for someone else, and it is, moreover, a little too early for sympathy when it is not yet known who is really going to need it.'

Thelma Thatcher (at least by squatter's rights) was smoking a cigarette in a long holder, and she took a deep breath of smoke and held it for a moment in her lungs and let it escape slowly between her lips as she examined Sid intently. She was rather tall and angular, with large hands and feet and a long upper lip that gave her a kind of squirrelly look. She must have represented, Sid thought, a radical reaction from Beth. Old simple Wilson, having had too much of one extreme, had palpably taken on too much of the other. Now she began to frown, in no mood for amenities, and this suited Sid exactly, for neither was she.

'Perhaps we had all better sit down,' Wilson Thatcher said.

'No, thank you,' Thelma Thatcher said. 'I don't wish to.'

'I don't either,' Sid said.

'It is evident from her use of my maiden name,' Thelma Thatcher said, 'that she intends to exploit certain information that was foolishly divulged to her, and I think she had better tell us exactly what she wants.'

'What I want,' Sid said, 'is simply to get Gid out of jail, where he has been put by a pair of idiots without a brain between them, even if it means putting someone else there in his place.'

'You seem to feel that we are in a position to help you. Please tell me how.'

'You can help me by telling the truth, that's how. Gid is in jail on suspicion of murder, simply because he happened to be in the place where the murder was supposedly done within the time some doctor thinks it happened, and it was all in the paper for everyone to read, but there was nothing there, not a single damn word, about how Beth Thatcher, after letting Wilson commit bigamy, came here to blackmail one or both of you for it. In my opinion, that's as good a motive for committing a murder as being foolish enough to go somewhere you shouldn't have gone at a time when you had much better have been anywhere else.'

'We have no obligation to tell you anything whatever.'

'That's true. But it may turn out to be more a matter of self-interest than obligation. It's easy to see that you are being protected by the authorities from public embarrassment, and if you don't want me to tell everything I know to everyone I meet, you'll damn well humor me in all that I ask.'

'It's apparent that you have no sense of decency.'

'That's right. All I have is Gid in jail, and I want him out.'

'What do you want to know?' Wilson Thatcher said.

'What I want to know,' Sid said, 'is exactly what Beth wanted from one or both of you. Besides that, I want to know why you came deliberately to our house and told us a lot of things that there was no need to tell anyone, let alone us, and which were probably lies.'

'I came and told you what I did,' Wilson said, 'because I was afraid. To be completely honest, I was afraid my wife had made a tragic mistake, and I was merely trying to divert to myself suspicions that I erroneously thought would fall upon her.'

'I prefer to judge for myself,' Sid said,

'whether they were erroneous or not.'

'I didn't want to go directly to the authorities,' Wilson said, 'because I thought they might consider it odd for me to confess so much when it was not necessary. I wanted them to know, however, in order to keep their attention away from my wife, and so I chose to tell Gideon. I did so for two reasons. In the first place, he was the one person, aside from me, who would have the greatest personal interest in Beth's death. In the second place, as a lawyer, he was someone I could talk to under the pretense of seeking advice. As you guessed, I told several lies. I suppose I was pretty transparent.'

'What you were,' Thelma Thatcher said, 'was a fool.'

'If so,' Sid said, 'he had lots of company.'

'I am finding this conversation exceedingly unpleasant,' Thelma Thatcher said, 'and I would like to end it. Wilson, if you will kindly keep quiet, I'm sure I can relate what happened much more quickly and clearly than you would find possible.'

'Quickly and clearly is the way I want it,' Sid said, 'whoever relates it.'

'Very well.' Thelma Thatcher drew smoke through her cigarette and detoured a little of it out through her nostrils, which gave her an effect, Sid thought, of angry belligerence, as if she were about to paw the carpet with her feet and suddenly charge someone. 'I'll tell you exactly what happened, regardless of what Wilson may have said in his ridiculous attempt to be heroic and sacrificial and divert suspicion to himself that was not yet directed toward anyone. This precious little bitch who was his first wife came to town, as you know, and one of the first things she did, apparently, was to call Wilson at his office and try to arrange a meeting with him, but he had the good sense to refuse to see her, fortunately, and I must admit that it was the only occasion in this whole affair when he showed any sense whatever. I doubt that she was greatly disappointed, however, for it was I she really wanted to see.

'She was shrewd enough in her way, and she was certain that she would be able to deal with me more easily and profitably than with Wilson. As a woman with a sense of shame and considerable pride, I would be almost certainly willing to pay handsomely to avoid being publicly humiliated and disgraced, whereas Wilson is reluctant to pay anything for any reason unless interest or dividends are assured.

'She came here to see me without even calling in advance, just as you have done, and there was no doubt that she was telling the truth about never having gotten the divorce, for she had all the details on the tip of her tongue and even invited me to check the records in the place where the divorce had supposedly been granted.

'She spoke as if it were all a kind of party game which everyone should accept in the best of humor, and then she said she only wanted twenty thousand dollars to go away. She promised to go somewhere and finally get a genuine divorce, after which Wilson and I could get quietly married again, and everything would be all right. She seemed to feel that she was making a very modest request as a special concession.'

'It wasn't necessary to give her a cent,' Wilson said. 'There wasn't a thing she could have done that wouldn't have been more unpleasant for her than for us.'

'Is that your opinion?' Thelma Thatcher said. 'I'm sure it is, for I've heard it at least a hundred times before. And I've explained patiently at least as many times that I am naturally reluctant to be known publicly as an extra-legal concubine to a bigamist, and it would have been very little consolation or comfort merely to have a treacherous little bitch suffering her own consequences in her own way at the same time. I preferred to pay the money, and I did. At least five thousand dollars of it. I happened to have that much in the house for a particular reason that is not relevant, and I gave it to her with the promise that I would give her the rest that night.

'In return, she promised that she would go away the very next day and get a real divorce quietly as soon as possible, and odd as it may seem under the circumstances, I somehow believed her. She left then, and I went to the bank and got the fifteen thousand from my personal account. It may seem like a lot of money to give someone, especially with no guarantee that she wouldn't be back for more, but I didn't believe that she would. Anyhow, twenty thousand dollars isn't *really* very much money to Wilson and me, however much it may be to some people. I'm sure that Wilson could have found some way to deduct most of it from his income tax as some kind of allowable expenditure. He's very clever at such things.'

'I don't think we'd better talk too much about that,' Wilson said.

'What I want to know,' Sid said, 'is if she came back for the rest of the money.'

'No, she didn't. I told her to come around nine, for I knew Wilson had a business meeting and wouldn't be home at that time. I had the money, and I waited for her, but she didn't come, and now, of course, it is apparent why she didn't.'

'Is it?' Sid said. 'Why didn't she?'

'Because she was murdered and couldn't.'

'It may be apparent to you, but it isn't

to me. I confess, in fact, that I am more than a little puzzled. She called Gid at nine-thirty, which was half an hour after she was supposed to have come here for the money, and I would like to know why the hell she was fooling around making a date with my husband and neglecting business in hand that was a lot more urgent and important.'

'I know nothing about that, but I do know that I've told the truth about my part in what happened here between me and her. Anything that Wilson said may be discounted as nonsense.'

'Well,' Wilson said, 'after she was killed and you told me about her being here, and for what reason, I admit I thought you might have killed her yourself, and it was my duty as a husband to protect you at my own expense, if possible.'

He looked forlorn and sounded pathetic, as if he expected to be commended instead of criticized, but Sid and Thelma Thatcher, who were incompatible relative to everything else, were agreed at least on the position that far too much idiocy had been excused on the grounds of good intentions, and their mutual attitude was primarily critical.

'Darling,' Thelma Thatcher said, 'it was just too manly of you.'

'And why,' Sid said, 'are you now so sure that what you originally thought wasn't perfectly correct?'

'As to that,' Thelma Thatcher said, 'it is probable that the murderer has already been found.'

'If I were in your place,' Sid said, 'I'm sure I would find it comforting to think so. I'd still like to know, however, why someone with fifteen thousand dollars waiting for her did not even take the trouble to pick it up before getting involved with someone else's husband, and incidentally with a murderer. In fact, I would like to know just where she went and what she did between the time she left Gid in the Kiowa Room and the time she went wherever she was killed and met whoever killed her.'

'Personally,' Thelma Thatcher said, 'I have no interest in that at all. If you want to know, why don't you go somewhere else and ask someone who might be able to tell you?'

'I intend to,' Sid said. 'Thank you for helping me, however reluctantly.'

'Not at all. I only hope that you will keep your part of the agreement and not expose us to public humiliation for an unfortunate mistake that was in no way our fault, except to the extent, perhaps, that Wilson was at fault in being incredibly gullible from first to last.'

'Was there an agreement? I don't recall any. To tell the truth, I am no more concerned about your difficulty, or the humiliation you may suffer as a consequence, than you are about getting Gid out of jail. It's largely a matter of one's interests, isn't it? However, I won't tell anyone about you immediately, or ever if it isn't necessary for Gid's sake. If it is, I'll tell whatever I know wherever it will do the most good.'

She turned and walked out into the hall, Wilson loping after her to the door and holding it for her as she left.

'Every word Thelma told you is perfectly true,' Wilson said. 'I assure you it is.'

'For the sake of your privacy,' Sid said, 'let us hope so.'

Driving downtown, she reviewed events as Thelma Thatcher had related them, and although she had perversely refused to admit it to the Thatchers, she was convinced, in fact, that every word of the version was true. She was convinced of this simply because it so perfectly accorded with her own preconceived notions of what had probably happened, which she had expressed, indeed, to Cotton McBride himself on the afternoon of Saturday last.

When she got downtown, she parked in the lot beside the Hotel Carson and went into the lobby. The clerk at the desk was young and overflowing with ideas and the juices of glands, both of which were stimulated by Sid, who was an adequate stimulant at all times and an expert one when she gave it her full attention. She was compelled to do so in this instance because the clerk, although susceptible, was reluctant to give out information about a guest, even a dead one, that might be considered confidential, especially to a woman, however stimulating, who happened to be the wife of the man who was suspected of having made the guest dead.

Finally, though, with hope high and hormones flowing, he confided that Beth Thatcher had checked her key at the desk late in the afternoon before the night she was killed, and that she had not picked it up again, and therefore could be assumed never to have returned to her room. Wherever she had gone, whatever to do, she had apparently gone directly from the Kiowa Room after drinking gimlets with Gideon Jones, and this was what Sid had wanted to know, and she went, knowing it, to see Chauncy at the bar.

A pair of waitresses were laying out the buffet in the lounge, and Chauncy's attitude indicated disapproval.

Aloof and scornful behind the bar, he expressed in his withdrawal a deep conviction that luncheon buffets were an intolerable intrusion that attracted the excessive patronage of women, who were collateral intruders tending to complicate life by ordering fancy concoctions that were difficult and time-consuming to mix, and were not, besides, fit to drink.

Chauncy was, in fact, a Swiss chocolate anachronism with a profound and mute longing for an earlier and simpler day of nickel beers and brass rails and men only, when lunch was served, if served at all, properly at the bar as a house treat for paying customers. This mute longing was not based on simple memory, for Chauncy was hardly old enough to remember the time when such conditions prevailed. It went much deeper than that. It was a kind of vestigial ache, scarcely diagnosed for what it was and passed along in mystic transmission from primitive ancestral bartenders.

Sid sat on a stool at the bar and claimed his attention. The soft light of appreciation in his limpid eyes was qualified by the unfortunate fact that she was a woman out of place, but that it was there at all was at the same time a concession, aesthetically, to the kind of woman she was. Chauncy had a pure and lustless love of pretty things that simple looking satisfied, and his sterner convictions could always be compromised by anything in this category — a bottle, an electric beer sign, a certain face. He moved into position opposite Sid, brown hands with polished nails placed flat on the bar.

'Yes, ma'am?'

'I believe I'll have a bourbon on the rocks, if you please.'

The stark simplicity of the order spoke well for the quality of her character, and Chauncy, after filling it, lingered in the vicinity and watched her discreetly.

'Do you know who I am?' she said.

'Yes, ma'am. Some faces I forget easy, and some I forget hard.'

'Well, what an absolutely nice thing to say. I think. Did you mean it as a compliment?'

'I meant it kindly as a fact, ma'am.'

'Do you know something, Chauncy? I have a notion that you are an exceptional person. Do you mind my calling you Chauncy?'

'No, ma'am. Chauncy's my name, and I expect to be called by it.'

'I've often heard my husband speak highly of you, and now I can understand why.'

'Mr. Gideon Jones is a generous gentleman. We've had many pleasant discussions.'

'I suppose you know that he's been put into jail.'

'I'm sorry, ma'am. An egregious error, I'm sure.'

'Did you know the lady he's suspected erroneously of killing?'

'Only by name and reputation. I remember her from years ago and from the recent evening she was here.'

'The evening she drank gimlets with Mr. Jones?'

'Yes, ma'am. An innocent episode, I assure you. She asked Mr. Jones to buy her the gimlet, which he did. They talked a while at a table, and Mr. Jones left alone.'

'I know. I don't suspect Mr. Jones of anything more than a kind of amiable and temporary soft-headedness, Chauncy, and so you needn't try to protect him. The lady is the one I'm interested in at the moment, and I wonder if you can remember how long she was here after Mr. Jones left.'

'I can estimate, if you like.'

'Please do.'

'Between half an hour and an hour. I regret that I can't be more exact.'

'When it comes to that, Chauncy, you are a good deal more exact than doctors and coroners. Thank you very much.'

'I'm pleased to be of help, ma'am.'

'Do you remember if she was alone all that time?'

'Oh, no. She was not alone. Several people stopped at her table to speak with her, and one or two, as I recall, sat with her until she left.'

'When she left, did she leave alone?'

'I think not. I have a vague remembrance of someone accompanying her.'

'But you're not sure?'

'That's correct. I'm not sure.'

'That's too bad, Chauncy. I wish you could be.'

'I'm sorry to disappoint you, ma'am.'

'You shouldn't be. I have no right to expect too much, and you are doing wonderfully well as it is. Does your vague remembrance of someone accompanying her include a vague remembrance of who that someone might have been?'

'No, ma'am. It doesn't, and it's odd, for you'd think it would.'

'How do you explain that it doesn't?'

'As I said, some faces you remember easy and some you remember hard. This is due, I believe, to the nature of pleasure. Your face, for example, if you will excuse me, is a face that gives one pleasure to remember, and it is therefore remembered easily and easily visualized, so that it can be seen at will in the imagination when one needs the refreshment of something good to look at.'

'It's wholly unnecessary, Chauncy, to ask to be excused for saying something like that.'

'I'm happy that you're not offended, ma'am.'

'On the contrary, I'm delighted. Are you sure you're not just being exceptionally nice? Do you actually sometimes look at my face in your imagination?'

'I have done so in the past, and I hope I may be permitted to continue.'

'Not only are you permitted, Chauncy, you are urged. Here and now you have permission to look at my face in your imagination whenever it pleases you.'

'Thank you. I'll be most circumspect as to time and place.'

'Is it your judgment, then, that you may not remember the person who may have left here with Beth Thatcher because the person may have a face that it doesn't please you to remember?'

'That's my judgment, ma'am, for what it's worth. I call it selective memory, and I believe that it becomes highly developed in certain of us who serve in positions that deny us the right to be discriminatory in our contacts. If I may say so, I would bear a heavy burden if I were unable to expunge immediately from my memory about 90 percent of the people I serve.'

'You may certainly say so, Chauncy, and I admire you for saying it. You're a gentleman and a philosopher of the highest order, and it has been a pleasure to talk with you.'

'The pleasure was mine, ma'am, and I hope Mr. Gideon Jones is soon released from jail.'

On this elevated plane of mutual respect, which was genuine, Sid and Chauncy parted, and Sid came on over to the county jail to see me. It was almost one o'clock when she got there, and I was full of chicken-fried steak and cream gravy when she arrived. I won't go into the details of what was said and done, the little of either that was possible under the imposed conditions, except that it was permitted to go on for quite a long time, thanks to a feeling of prejudice in our favor held by Harley Murchison, who had beat me at dominoes last night and was looking forward to beating me again after supper was served later.

She reported the events of the day, which I have set down in action and dialogue dressed up a little by imagination within the bounds of possibility, if not probability, and then, after a eulogy of Chauncy's superior character and intellect, we said goodbye again with restrained fervor, and she went home.

She was tired and sticky after a busy time on a hot day, and she went upstairs and had a shower and lay down on the bed in our room to think about what she had learned and where she now was in relation to it, and where she was, so far as she could see, was somewhat behind where she had been when she started.

As stated, she was convinced that Thelma Thatcher had told the truth, inasmuch as it confirmed Sid's own notions. She was also convinced that Wilson Thatcher had not been foolish enough to kill anyone over a matter that could have been settled much less dangerously otherwise, although Wilson's potential for foolishness was demonstrably considerable, and that left me out in front all alone, in jail and available. This trend of thought left her feeling depressed and inadequate and wanting to cry, and so she cursed a little and closed her eyes and took several deep breaths and went sound asleep.

To her surprise, when she woke, it was quite late, going on six, and she began at once to understand from a hollow ache in her stomach that she was in need of food, if not actually hungry. She had another shower, a quick one, and pulled on a shirt and a pair of shorts and went downstairs to the kitchen, where she found cold roast beef for a sandwich and cold milk to drink with it. She would have preferred beer to the milk, but one beer generally led to several, as she knew from experience, and she needed a clear head to think with. After eating the beef sandwich and drinking the cold milk, she went with her clear head out onto the back terrace.

The day had cooled off, and there was a soft breeze, and she sat there in the breeze and began trying to think, but it was rather futile, all thoughts coming to nothing new, and then suddenly she remembered that tomorrow night was the night of the meeting of the discussion group, at which she and Rose Pogue were to discuss Zoroaster, and she realized that it would be absolutely impossible for her to go. It would be necessary for her to tell Rose at once, so that Rose could plan to do everything as best she could alone. It would be placing Rose in a difficult position, of course, but, then, Rose was intellectual and ingenious, and would manage very well to fill in Sid's time with only a little advance notice.

Getting up, Sid went inside to the telephone in the hall and dialed Rose's number.

'Hello,' she said. 'Is that you, Rose?'

'Yes,' Rose said. 'It's Sid, isn't it?'

'Yes, it is,' Sid said, 'and I should have called you sooner, but it simply didn't enter my mind.'

'Where on earth have you been all day? I've tried and tried without success to reach you.'

'I've been busy investigating things, but I must say that I haven't gotten much of anywhere with it.'

'Well, darling, I was simply thunder-struck when I read in the papers what had happened to Gid, and I only wanted to say that if there is the slightest thing I can do to help, you mustn't hesitate to call on me.'

'There *is* something, actually, and that's really what I've called about. I've just remembered the discussion group tomorrow night, and I can't be there. Would you mind doing it alone?'

'I won't say that I wouldn't mind ordinarily, but under the circumstances it can hardly be helped. With Gid in jail, you can't be expected to engage effectively in a discussion of Zoroaster.'

'It's very kind of you, Rose. I'm sorry to leave you in such a fix.'

'No, no, darling. You are not to let it distress you in the least. You already have enough on your mind as it is.'

'Thanks enormously, Rose. You're so clever about such things, I'm sure you'll manage beautifully without me.'

'Wait a minute. Don't hang up. Were you about to hang up?'

'I was about to, yes.'

'I wanted to ask you if matters will be cleared up shortly? Do you think so?'

'At first I thought so, but now I'm not quite so optimistic.'

'Surely he didn't do it?'

'Surely not.'

'What on earth could have made him go to the park?'

'He went to say goodbye to someone he had known well. It was perfectly understandable and perfectly innocent.'

'Do you think so? That's comforting, at least. I have been told that Beth Thatcher was quite attractive.'

'I only saw her dead, and she was beautiful.'

'How unusual. So often dead people aren't. Wasn't it the night you were over here that he went to see her?'

'Yes.'

'Darling, did you know he was going?'

'I didn't know it in advance, because he didn't know it himself until after I had left. He told me he had gone when I returned home.'

'Really? One always wonders about such things, doesn't one? I mean it could be either a sign of innocence or an exceptionally bold bit of deception. I will say, however, that you are being very steadfast and loyal, and I admire you for it.'

'I'm not being steadfast and loyal at all. I am only lonely and wanting Gid home. He isn't so much, perhaps, as men go, but he's mine, and I want to keep him.'

'Of course, darling. If that's what you want, I'm sure I want it for you. And you are not to worry about Zoroaster. Not for an instant.'

'Thanks again, Rose. Goodbye.'

On the back terrace, sitting and thinking with a clear head in the cool breeze, she reviewed once more her conversation with the Thatchers, but the prospects for anything enlightening coming from it grew dimmer and dimmer all the time, and in fact it was more confusing than otherwise, for it left her wondering, in the first place, how anyone as simple-minded as Wilson had ever managed to make so much money, and in the second, why in hell Beth Thatcher, who had called on the telephone about nine-thirty, had failed to pick up fifteen thousand dollars at nine when it had been agreed upon and arranged.

Arriving at no answers to these puzzlers, she began to think then about the conversation between Beth and me as I had related it, to see if anything significant could be detected there that had heretofore escaped detection. She had a good memory for details, and she began at the beginning, with the ringing of the phone, and went over them all carefully once, after which she began to go over them again.

The God damn treacherous cicadas were noisy in the trees. In the pale light, the moon was pale in the sky. In the backyard across the hedge, Jack Handy was watering the grass and making comments in a loud voice to Mrs. Jack Handy, who was apparently somewhere in the house. On a near street, moving rapidly, was the tinkling sound of the siren bell of a Good-Humor man. They drove around in little jeeps painted white nowadays, the Good-Humor men did. Not in little wagons drawn by a horse as they used to do.

'Why,' said Sid suddenly, 'it's absurd! It's simply absurd!'

She was on her feet with a sense of rising excitement, and she felt in an instant much better than she had been feeling.

Feeling so good, and now having no longer such a pressing need of a clear head, she went inside and mixed three Martinis and brought them out and drank them.

13

'Sugar,' Sid said, 'last night I was thinking and thinking, and finally I thought of something enlightening.'

'Is that so?' I said. 'I've been thinking and thinking too, and the result has been almost precisely the opposite.'

I looked out the window into the yard beneath the spreading trees. The grass was dark green and cool-looking and inviting, and I wished I could go out and roll in it like a dog. It was my third day in jail, and I was tired of it. I wanted to go home.

'Well,' she said, 'this enlightening thing is something that was said, and it was said, moreover, directly to you. I don't want to be excessively critical, sugar, but it does seem to me that a lawyer should be a little more capable of analyzing things and seeing their significance and all that. Do you suppose you would have done better to be something else?'

'It's often occurred to me. Just recently, you'll remember, I went through a brief period of wanting to be a soldier of fortune or a deep sea fisherman or a Left Bank bum. Never mind that, however. Please tell me what was said that you've thought of that's enlightening.'

'I suppose I must, if you can't think of it yourself. To begin with, I've been greatly puzzled as to why Beth Thatcher was fooling around making a date with my husband when she should have been attending to more important business. It just didn't seem sensible, and that's all there was to it.'

'I'm with you so far.'

'Then early last night I was out on the back terrace feeling depressed and lonely, and I suddenly remembered Rose Pogue and Zoroaster and the discussion group, which meets tonight. I couldn't possibly go, because of you in jail, and everything being in such a mess, and so I called Rose and told her I couldn't, and that got me to thinking about the telephone conversation you had with Beth, it being the same night I went to Rose's, and all at once, after I had thought for a while, it was perfectly clear to me why Beth had neglected her business to make a date with you.'

'Was it? Is it? Not to me. Why?'

'Because she didn't.'

'Didn't? Didn't what?'

'Didn't make a date with you.'

'I'm sorry to be contrary, but she did. She called me on the telephone. I was drinking gimlets and listening to 'Death and Transfiguration' at the time. I've told you and told you and told you.'

'I know, sugar. I know *someone* called you, that is. But what makes you so positive it was Beth?'

'Because she said it was.'

'Anyone could have said it. That doesn't make it so.'

'Look, Sid, it won't do. Honestly it won't. Beth had a voice that sounded like an invitation to bed if she so much as asked for a light. There was no other voice like it that I ever heard, and I'd have recognized it anytime, anywhere.'

'Please don't be so obtuse, sugar. You have scarcely covered yourself with distinction in this matter up to now, as I've pointed out before, and its time you made a special effort to do a little better. Surely you can see that the unusual quality of Beth's voice is precisely the thing that would make it so easy to imitate. I mean, a common sort of voice would be quite difficult, really, but almost anyone with a little effort could do Donald Duck or Tallulah Bankhead.'

'Are you saying that someone called me and pretended to be Beth?'

'Yes, sugar. It explains other things and must be true.'

'What makes you think it's true? You haven't given me any reason yet.'

'I was in hopes you'd get it without my help. It would restore my confidence in you somewhat if you could. Can't you? Really try.'

'Damn it, Sid, cut it out. I'm in no mood to match wits with you this afternoon. I concede defeat.'

'Oh, well, it's evident that you are determined not to see what is perfectly clear. I may as well tell you, I suppose. It was what was said about Rose Pogue that makes me sure it was not Beth Thatcher who said it. I'm ashamed that I didn't understand it sooner.'

'All I can remember being said about Rose Pogue was that a conference with her might go on and on forever. That was after I had said you'd gone over to talk with her about Zoroaster and had left me alone.'

'There! You see, sugar? You only needed to make a genuine effort, and you thought of it right away. You are not really so obtuse as you sometimes seem.'

'Thank you. Now that I've thought of it, perhaps you'll tell me what the hell in particular it means.'

'Why, sugar, how could Beth Thatcher have possibly known that Rose is so talkative and goes on and on forever about matters in detail? After all, Beth Thatcher left town seven years ago, and Rose only came three years ago, when she was hired by the Board of Education to teach second grade, and it was therefore clearly impossible for Beth to know Rose at all, or anything whatever about her.'

She was sitting on the long table with

her legs hanging over the edge, and her eyes were bright with pride and excitement. I had been standing facing her, but now I felt limp all of a sudden, as if my bones had gone soft in an instant, and I sank down slowly onto a straight chair and put my forehead against her knees and closed my eyes.

'Sugar,' she said, 'are you all right?'

'All right,' I said, and I had this assured feeling that she was truly onto something of significance, and that all right everything would shortly be, if it wasn't quite already. 'I'm only wondering who it could have been. Who, conceivably, could it have been?'

'There is nothing difficult about that,' Sid said. 'It was whoever killed her, of course.'

'And who, conceivably, is whoever killed her?'

'As to that, I'm not sure yet, but there are things that can be safely deduced, and the first deduction is that the killer is surely a woman. As I told you, it would have been easy for a woman to imitate Beth's voice, even if she were no more

261

than a little clever, but it would hardly have been possible for a man, unless he were especially talented and trained, which isn't likely.'

'That sounds reasonable enough. Now go on deducing. Deduce, for example, why this woman, whoever she may be, killed Beth and then tricked me into going to Dreamer's Park and incriminating myself.'

'Why, sugar, that is so elementary that it doesn't really deserve to be called deducing. Allowing for the possibility of her being a little crazy, which could have been a factor, she undoubtedly killed Beth because she hated her, and incriminated you because she hated you also, although not quite so much, perhaps, as Beth. The incrimination part was kind of sloppy and uncertain at best. There was no assurance that it would work, and it nearly didn't, for you simply kept quiet about finding the body, which you might not have found at all in such a dark place, and it looked as though you were going to come out of it with no more than a certain amount of inconvenience and a somewhat guilty conscience. That is why, after a while, it was necessary to send the note to the police.'

'You contend, then, that the telephoner and the writer are one and the same person?'

'Oh, yes. Naturally. It's practically certain.'

'By God, it's almost traumatic to feel that one's been the cause of such machinations. I can understand someone's wanting to kill Beth, for I've felt the desire myself on occasion, but I can't quite see myself as the kind of fellow who incites such strong emotion.'

'Sugar, I'm prepared to testify that you are perfectly capable of inciting strong emotion, but that is beside the present point, and we'd better not get into it. What we must get into is who this woman is by name, and I'm just beginning to get some interesting ideas that may amount to something. As I recall, regarding your telephone conversation, you said you were drinking gimlets, and whoever was imitating Beth said something about drinking gimlets *still*. Is that true?'

'Yes. True. I remember distinctly. And I said not still, but again, because of the bottle of wine.'

She was swinging her legs now like a small, intense girl watching a foot race or something else exciting, and her face was set in the fiercest imaginable scowl of concentration.

'It's apparent, then, that the person on the telephone, who was surely a woman, was also someone who knew that you had been drinking gimlets. Since it has been established that it was not Beth, it must have been someone else who was right there in the Kiowa Room watching you at the time, and there is only one person that I can remember your mentioning by name when you came home late and covered me with gin kisses on the terrace.'

She stopped swinging her legs and sat very still on the table, and the fierce scowl faded slowly through subtle changes into an expression of childish wonder.

'Sugar,' she said, 'why would Sara Pike want to kill Beth Thatcher and go to all sorts of extremes to put the blame on you?'

'*Sara Pike!* Are you serious, Sid? You can't be.'

'I can and I am. Now that I've thought it through and come to a solution, I have an absolute conviction. Please answer my question. What did you and Beth Thatcher ever do to Sara Pike?'

'Nothing. Nothing at all.'

'There you go. Answering again before thinking. Half of your troubles, I'm sure, come from talking or acting without thinking first. Of course you did something to her, however unintentional it may have been. It's a simple matter of being reasonable. She certainly didn't kill Beth and incriminate you for nothing at all.'

'Well, I can't think of anything. Not a damn thing.'

'Isn't it true that Beth and Sara's brother Sherman once went together seriously?'

'Yes. That's true enough.'

'And isn't it also true that she broke off with him and took up with you after you got back from being away?'

'True, true, but of damn little consequence.'

'Perhaps. We'll continue to think about it and see. At any rate, you said you had done nothing, and already we have come up with something.'

'I said nothing was done to Sara. What was done to Sherm was something else, and it really amounted to damn little. Sherm was a brilliant sort of guy, and a nice one. No hard feelings. Besides, he died right away, and none of it made any difference to him then, one way or another.'

'Well, there it is, sugar. You have said it yourself.'

'Said what?'

'That he died right away. Dying is surely something.'

'Oh, come off it, Sid. He'd had rheumatic fever as a kid. He died of heart failure.'

'Are you sure? Who said so?'

'The doctor said so, that's who.'

'Who was the doctor? Do you remember?'

'Yes, I do. Old Doctor Weinsap is who. He was the Pike's family doctor, and he was ours too. I think he was damn near everyone's family doctor.'

'I don't know any Doctor Weinsap. Is he still practicing?'

'Not here, at least. He's dead.'

'That's too bad, for I would like to talk with him. Anyhow, it's well known that old family doctors are inclined to make mistakes, and sometimes they will even say deliberately, out of a feeling of affection, that dying was the result of one thing when it was actually the result of something else entirely. I know this is true because I had an uncle on my mother's side who died of acute alcoholism, and the family doctor, who was a friend, put it on the death certificate as some kind of kidney trouble.'

'So far as that goes, alcoholism and kidney trouble are frequently connected. Nevertheless, with all due respect to your mother's brother, there is no reason whatever to suspect that Sherm Pike died of anything but what Doctor Weinsap said he died of.'

'You're far too credulous, sugar. You'll believe anything fantastic, even when the truth is as clear as can be.'

'I'm sorry. What, precisely, is the truth?'

'The truth is that Sherman Pike committed suicide. That's perfectly evident.'

'Is it? Why?'

'Because of what has happened, of course. It's the one thing that would explain why Sara Pike would do what she has to Beth Thatcher and you.'

'I'm not sure, but something in your reasoning seems wrong. It's backwards or something. Maybe you're starting with a basic assumption that isn't proved.'

'You had better leave the reasoning to me, sugar. You'll have to admit that I've been more successful at it to this point than you have been. You'll see. It will turn out that Sherman Pike committed suicide in some way because Beth Thatcher threw him over for you, and all this time Sara Pike has been brooding about it, knowing the truth, and when Beth came back to town, Sara met her and suddenly cracked up and killed her. Probably she has become somewhat crazy from keeping all this inside her for so long. Something like that is extremely hard on the mind.

Everyone knows it.'

'Sara took Sherm's death hard, all right, but that was natural. He was a little older than she, a brilliant, sensitive guy with a good future, as everyone thought, and she was nuts about him. For a long time after he died, she was practically a recluse. Never went anywhere or saw anyone.'

'There you are again. You keep trying to argue one way, but everything you say goes the other. No, no, sugar, you can't dissuade me. Sara Pike did it and tried to put the blame on you, I'm certain of that now, and it only remains to find out exactly how.'

'Yes? It seems to me that it also remains to prove it.'

'You're right for once. Idiots like Hector Caldwell and Cotton McBride must have everything done for them completely. Don't worry, however. Now that I've begun so well and gone so far, I'll surely think of a way to finish successfully.'

She was still sitting there on the table with her legs hanging over, and I was still in the chair, although I had removed my head from her knees some time ago, when she had started to swing her legs and concentrate, and I got up and walked over to the window and looked out at the place under the trees where the two boys had been, but were not now, and after a while I turned and went back to where she was standing, having slipped off the edge of the table while I was gone.

'Look,' I said. 'Will you do something for me? Will you please do it?'

'I may and I may not. It depends.'

'If you love me a little yet, in spite of everything, you'll do it.'

'As a matter of fact, I love you a great deal yet, in spite of everything, and so if I will do it if I love you, I suppose I'll do it.'

'All right. Go home. Go home and say a prayer or curse or cry, but let me come out of this in my own way. Nothing can be proved against me, and it's only a matter of time until I'll be released.'

'Do you really want me to?'

'I do. I really do.'

'It's plain that you have no faith in me.'

'I just don't want you to get hurt or into trouble.'

'I thought I was doing so well, too.'

'You've done fine, and I appreciate it, but now it's time to let someone else do the rest.'

'All right. I can see that it's no use. It was foolish of me to try.'

It was time for her to go, and she went as far as the door, where she stopped. She looked very small and somehow beaten, looking back, and there was something shining in her eyes.

'God damn son of a bitch,' she said.

And then she left, but she didn't go home. She went, instead, to the office, where Millie Morgan was.

'Hello, there, Sid,' Millie said. 'How's the investigation going?'

'It's going very well, as a matter of fact. For a while it hardly went at all, but then it began going better, and now it's practically finished. Are you still available?'

'Yes, I am. I was about to ask if you couldn't make some use of me. There's very little to do around here right now,

271

and I'm getting bored. I was even considering asking my engineer in for a scrimmage. What do you want me to do?'

'First I had better brief you on my conclusions. From several things that were said, it became apparent that the person who called Gid on the telephone and arranged to meet him in Dreamer's Park was not Beth Thatcher, as the person claimed, but someone else who knew Rose Pogue, which Beth didn't. It was easy to understand from this that Beth was dead at the time of the call, already killed, and that whoever called had killed her and wanted to incriminate Gid if possible out of pure spite. It's my opinion at present that the killing was done somewhere besides the park, and the body taken there afterward. From some other significant things that I won't bother to explain just now, it was easy to decide who did the killing and the telephoning, and probably even why they were done, but the trouble as matters now stand is that I can't prove it.'

'Proof would be helpful. I can see that.'

'It will be absolutely essential, to be

realistic, and the only way I can think of to prove it is to get a confession by some kind of deception, and that's why I've come to consult you. The one thing that is perfectly obvious is that it's of no use to expect any contributions from Cotton McBride or Hec Caldwell.'

'You did just right in coming to me. I'm pretty good at deception, and I may be able to help you work something out. Incidentally, am I allowed to know who did the killing?'

'By all means. Didn't I say? It was Sara Pike who did it.'

'The hell she did! It's almost incredible. What makes you think so?'

'Well, I don't want to take the time to go into it fully, but Sherman Pike, who was supposed to have died of heart failure, didn't die of heart failure at all, but killed himself because Beth Thatcher left him and took up with Gid again. It was kept a secret all this time, but Sara knew it and brooded about it, and so, when she just recently got her first chance, she managed to kill Beth and incriminate Gid out of revenge. As I

273

admitted, I can't prove any of it yet, but it's perfectly apparent.'

'It is? Tell me why.'

'Oh, because Sara knew Gid had been drinking gimlets in the Kiowa Room, and was surely the one on the telephone, and was just as surely, therefore, the one who did the killing. She had to have a reason for killing Beth and calling Gid, of course, and the only reason that seems probable is the one I've just explained. You see now? It's perfectly apparent.'

'It does become clearer when you know all the facts. How do you propose to deceive Sara into confessing?'

'That's what we must now put our minds to, and I have a plan already thought out that I'd like to have your opinion of.'

'Tell me the plan, and I'll give you my opinion gladly.'

'We must keep in mind, to begin with, that someone who has killed someone is bound to be uneasy and afraid of the possible consequences, which will make her extremely susceptible to suggestions and threats and things like that. What I propose to do, if you agree, is to call Sara without identifying myself and claim to have seen her commit the murder. She will certainly deny at first that she did it, of course, but I'll convince her one way or another that I happened by accident to see her, and what I intend to do then is pretend to be a blackmailer who wants money to keep quiet about it, just as Beth actually was in connection with something that I've promised not to tell about unless necessary. I'll arrange to meet her alone at some place where you can be hiding as a witness, unknown to her, and it will be up to me to get her to convict herself by what she says, although the simple fact that she comes to meet me will surely be evidence of her guilt.'

'Do you think I'll be acceptable to Hec Caldwell as a witness? I doubt it. He'll be likely to believe that we've made it all up just to get Gid out of jail.'

'He may be a little dubious, I admit, but he will certainly have to make an investigation of Sara as a result, and once he and Cotton McBride are put on to her, even they may discover the truth. It's probable that Sara's somewhat unstable mentally and will break down and admit everything soon enough if seriously accused.'

'Nevertheless, I think it might be a good idea to have one or both of them there to hear it with me.'

'I've thought of that, but I don't believe I want to risk it. I'm afraid they might reject the plan and refuse to let us go through with it.'

'Another thing that bothers me a little is the feeling that it might be dangerous. Sara's probably unstable, as you say, to have done such a thing, and in fact I consider it likely that she may be secretly as mad as the March Hare. There's no telling what she may try to do to you, and to me also if I'm forced to come to your assistance.'

'There's some danger in it, all right, but I'm prepared to face it for Gid's sake.'

'Well, I'm not quite so dedicated to Gid as you are, but I'm willing to face it with you. When do you intend to call Sara?'

'Now is as good a time as any. Will you

please look up her number in the directory?'

Millie looked it up and told it to Sid, and Sid dialed. The phone at the other end of the line rang twice and was answered. It was answered by Sara, who lived alone.

'Is it Sara Pike speaking?' Sid said.

'Yes,' Sara said. 'Who's this?'

'You don't know me, but I know you, and I know what you've done because I saw you do it.'

'What's that? What did you say?'

Sara's voice, Sid said later, was suddenly shrill and almost frenzied, and it was obvious immediately that she was, as Sid had predicted, extremely susceptible to suggestions and oblique threats and things like that.

'You heard what I said, and you know what I mean,' Sid said.

'On the contrary, I don't understand you at all. Tell me who you are and what you want. Why have you called me?'

'I've called to tell you that I saw you kill Beth Thatcher. I was there and saw it, and you had better believe me. Don't hang up, or I'll go straight to the police.'

'Are you insane?'

'I'm not, but I think that you may be.'

'What do you want?'

'We had better meet somewhere and talk about that.'

'I'm not at all sure that I agree. Why should I?'

'For the same reason that you haven't hung up. To keep me from going to the police.'

'I don't even know who you are. Are you afraid to tell me your name?'

'You'll know me when you see me, and that will be soon enough. Do you agree now to meet me? If you don't, I'll hang up myself, and you can take the consequences.'

There was a long silence on the line, and Sid had an uneasy feeling that there was a great deal of furious thinking going on at the other end, thinking that was probably not quite sane but crazy-crafty, and this turned out to be true from what was next said.

'I'll meet you in one place only,' Sara said. 'It must be there or nowhere.'

'Where is that?' Sid said.

'At the place where you say you saw me kill Beth Thatcher, and you must tell me right now where that place is.'

It was a neat and treacherous little trap, clearly one that Sid should have anticipated, and she cursed herself because she hadn't. She felt at once triumphant and defeated, for it was apparent that she had been right all the way along, that the murder had truly been done somewhere besides Dreamer's Park, and if she now said Dreamer's Park, which was where it was supposed to have been done, she would give herself away as a liar, but she didn't, of course, know where else to say. *But Sara knew where else.* That was equally apparent, and the little trap, however neat and deadly, was also a confession.

There was an even longer silence on the line now, but this time it was Sid who was doing the furious thinking. She explained afterward that it was like one of those odd psychological experiences in which someone in a great crisis is able to do something that would normally be impossible, like the man who picked up the safe that weighed five hundred pounds and threw it out the window of a burning building. Sid was not required to perform a physical feat, however.

She was only required to know in an instant where Sara Pike had killed Beth Thatcher, and it was actually a little longer than an instant before she knew, but she knew soon enough. All of a sudden, she was hearing Cotton McBride say again that the wound had really been a sort of puncture with a little dirt around the edge, and immediately after that she was standing beside me in the cemetery, helping bury Beth again, and she was seeing now what she had seen then without really noticing, and what she saw was a metal vase for flowers with a spike on the bottom that you push into the ground to keep the vase from falling over. She had, she said later, an exhilarating and immediate feeling of absolute assurance.

'Surely,' she said assuredly. 'I'll meet you beside your brother Sherman's grave.'

There was a third interval of silence. Then Sara's voice, curiously flat and almost apathetic.

'Shall we say about eight o'clock?'

'Eight o'clock will be fine,' Sid said.

She hung up with a feeling of having done quite well. In fact, she didn't know how she could have done much better.

'Sara's guilty, as I thought,' she said to Millie. 'We're going to meet at eight o'clock.'

'I would almost swear,' Millie said, 'that you said beside her brother Sherman's grave.'

'It was a trick on her part. I had to name the place where Beth was killed in order to prove I was not lying about seeing it done, which in fact I was.'

'How the hell did you know the place? Did you know it all along?'

'No. It just came to me suddenly when I remembered about the puncture and the dirt and the little metal vases with spikes in the cemetery.'

'Oh. That explains everything nicely. A cemetery seems an odd place for Beth to have gone with Sara Pike, however. Why do you suppose she went?'

'Well, Gid said Beth was very sentimental in her own way, and I agree that
she must have been. After all, she had
gone seriously once with Sherman Pike,
and she met Sara in the Kiowa Room,
and undoubtedly it all came back
nostalgically or something. It's not so
odd, really, that she went with Sara to
visit Sherman's grave, especially if Sara
suggested it. There are a few people I
have known who are dead and buried in
different places that I would gladly visit if
it were convenient.'

'That may be true, but I can think of
many places that I would prefer to a
cemetery as a place to meet someone who
has killed once and might not be averse to
killing again. Especially at eight o'clock.
Isn't it beginning to get pretty dark then?'

'That's only so much the better. I
prefer that she not recognize me until she
gets quite close.'

'Where, may I ask, am I supposed to be
hiding all this time?'

'I've considered that. The Pike plot, as I
recall, is right next to the Thatcher

mausoleum, and the mausoleum's just the place.'

'Oh, by God! If you imagine that I'm going to hide in a mausoleum at eight o'clock, you're simply mistaken. Or any other time, for that matter.'

'Not *in* it. *Behind* it. It would be impossible to get in it, anyhow, for it's naturally kept locked.'

'Well, behind it is bad enough, but I agree to hide there. What time shall we meet and go?'

'We had better go separately, I think, as a precaution. I'll go there directly by the main entrance to the cemetery, but you had better slip in at the far side near the mausoleum so as not to be seen. It will entail some walking through a field, for there is no road approaching on that side. You must give yourself time enough to be in position shortly before eight.'

'I'll be there,' Millie said. 'You can count on me.'

14

So there they were at eight o'clock, Sid beside Sherm's grave and Millie behind the Thatcher mausoleum.

And there at eight also, a thin and ghostly shape approaching slowly among the headstones, was Sara Pike.

She stopped when she was quite near and leaned forward to peer through the shadows. She was wearing a loose, light coat that hung freely from the shoulders, although it was a warm evening, and her hands were thrust deeply into the pockets of the coat.

'Who is it?' she said. 'It's Sydnie Jones, isn't it?'

'Yes, it is.'

'Why are you here? Was it you who called? It's a trick, isn't it?'

Her voice was thin and clear but somehow remote, as if it carried through the air from a great distance.

'It's no trick,' Sid said. 'I had to talk

with you, and I knew you would refuse if I merely asked.'

'Have you come here alone? You haven't, have you? Who is with you?'

'No one is with me, as you can see.'

'Are you sure? You could be lying. Perhaps someone is behind the mausoleum.'

'No one is there, but you can look if you like.'

'I think I shall. Please stand where you are while I do. I don't want you to come near me.'

It was a precarious moment for the plan, and Sid was depending heavily upon the sharp ears and physical agility of Millie, who did not disappoint her. When Sara was at the front end of the mausoleum, about to turn the corner to the opposite side, Millie popped into view at the rear end, and she kept popping around corners out of sight just ahead of Sara until the mausoleum had been circled entirely and she was back where she had started. The suspense to Sid was severe, but the sudden shock of seeing that Millie was not alone was even worse, and the person with her, popping around corners with an equal agility, was no one but Cotton McBride.

Sara, having circled the mausoleum, turned and came back toward Sid, stopping about six feet away, her hands still thrust deeply into the pockets of her light coat.

'You see?' Sid said. 'There is no one here but you and me.'

'Why do you want to talk with me? What do you want?'

'I want to talk with you because Gid, as you know, is in jail on suspicion of having killed Beth Thatcher, but he didn't do it, as you also know, because you did it yourself right here where we are.'

'Who says I did?'

'I say it.'

'You say it, but you can't prove it. You told me on the phone that you saw me, but you didn't. You have only made some guesses.'

'Deductions are what I've made, and they're true ones.'

'That doesn't matter. Even the truth must be proved. Who will believe that I did it? What reason did I have?'

'The reason is lying here between us, where he has lain for seven years.'

'Sherm? Do you mean Sherm? Yes, that's true. How do you know? More guesses?'

'More deductions. He killed himself, and it was covered up as heart failure, which was easy enough for everyone to accept, because he had had rheumatic fever as a boy.'

'You're very clever. You must be very clever indeed. But no matter. It's all true.'

Sara's voice took on a kind of singsong, crooning tone and tempo.

'He was tender and brilliant and very good, and I loved him more than anyone else in the world, more by far than everyone else put together, and then he deliberately killed himself with the sleeping medicine he sometimes used to take at nights. He went to sleep and never woke up, and the empty bottle was there beside him when I found him, and I hid the bottle and told the doctor he simply died in his sleep. I don't think the doctor believed it at all, but he was a friend of the family and pretended to believe it for our sake, and now he's dead too and can never say differently. So far as anyone will ever know, Sherm died in his sleep of a bad heart, but he really died of a bad woman, a pretty little whore. I loved him and would have taken care of him always, but he didn't want me, he wanted the whore instead and didn't want to live without her, and so he killed himself, killed himself over the whore, and left me all alone for all these years.'

'I'm sorry. Truly I am.'

'Don't dare to be sorry. I won't have you being sorry, for you are married to the man who was partly to blame, but now he is going to pay me back for it, even though Sherm wouldn't have wanted it this way, and then *I* will be sorry for *you*, but it won't make any difference.'

'Why should you hate Gid? He never deliberately hurt your brother or you or anyone else.'

'He took the little whore and made my brother die. Now I have killed the whore and destroyed her consort. The waiting was long, very long, but in the end it was so easy. She came here willingly with me, to visit the grave out of shallow sentiment, and I'm not really sure that I intended to kill her in the beginning. I only intended, I think, to tell her the truth. How Sherm died, and why, so that it would be on her conscience the rest of her life. That was foolish of me, wasn't it? To imagine that she would have a conscience?

'Do you know what she said when I told her? We were standing right here beside the grave, and I told her, and she said, *Well, what a perfectly ridiculous thing to do.* That was when I picked up the vase and stabbed her in the back. The Voice told me suddenly to do it. It was getting late, not quite so late as now, but getting dusk, and I had to do something with her, of course, and the Voice kept telling me what to do. First I hid her body over there in the tall grass of that field, but then I was told to take her to Dreamer's Park and incriminate her consort, who helped her kill my brother. I drove around as close as I could to where she was in the grass, and then I carried

289

her to the car and took her to the park and carried her in there and put her in the bandstand under the seat so that there would be little or no chance of the wrong person finding her too soon and ruining everything. It was quite a dangerous thing to do, I suppose, but ever so exciting and satisfying. She was quite easy to carry, for I am much stronger than I look, and it was even easier to deceive her consort later and persuade him to meet her there. He must be a very credulous person. A fool.'

'He had been drinking gimlets.'

'It looked for a while, however, as if things might go wrong after all. It looked as if the consort might escape suspicion, and so I wrote the note to the police, and now everything is working out beautifully as I wanted it to and as the Voice said it would.'

'Is it? Perhaps you are too optimistic.'

'Because of you? Oh, no. It was a mistake for you to come here, or to meddle at all, for now I must kill you, as you must surely see.'

'How? Is there a gun in one of your

pockets? Is that why you keep your hands there?'

'Not a gun. I know nothing about guns, and they're noisy besides. A knife. I can use a knife quite well. There is no use for you to scream, because there is no one to hear you, nor to run, because I can run faster, nor to struggle, because I am far stronger.'

'If you kill me, you will surely be caught.'

'No, no. Never. The Voice has assured me that I will not. The Voice comes to me and tells me what to do, and it is always right. It is a great advantage, having the Voice. Maybe it's the Voice of God. Someday it will tell me if it is or not, and in the meanwhile it has told me that you must be killed, and there's nothing you can do to prevent it, nothing at all.'

'As to that,' Sid said, 'it seems to me that I have already done more than my share, *and in my opinion it is high time that Cotton McBride begins doing his.*'

Cotton came out from behind the mausoleum then, on the run, and began doing his share to the best of his ability.

Sara shrieked and clawed and fiercely struggled, and it looked for a while as if Cotton would need the assistance of Sid and Millie, but then, all at once, Sara became perfectly quiet, orally and bodily, and stood looking with an air of abstraction across the clustered head-stones as if she were listening again to the Voice, which may have been telling her to give up.

'Damn it, Millie,' Sid said, 'I told you that Cotton was not to be in on it, but you brought him in anyhow, in spite of all my instructions.'

'Fortunately for both of us, I did,' Millie said. 'The more I thought about it, the more I was convinced that it would be helpful to have some muscles present, even of an idiot.'

'I admit that you were right,' Sid said, 'and I, for a change, was wrong.'

15

A few evenings later, we had a little party on the back terrace to celebrate my getting out of jail.

We had gimlets to drink because Sid said it was important that I not develop a thing about them.

In addition to Sid and me, Millie was there with her engineer, who was still trying desperately with a kind of restrained frenzy.

Hec Caldwell was there with his wife, just to show that there were no hard feelings, much.

Even Cotton McBride was there, a limp and lonely stag because he had never had any luck with the girls and still wasn't having any.

The Jack Handys were not invited, but they drifted around the hedge and got into it.

Everything is clear up to a point, and then nothing is, and what I remember most clearly is Sid saying that I had become much more interesting to her since she had discovered that I was once a whore's consort.

Another thing I remember pretty clearly is someone saying that he or she wondered what would become of Sara Pike, and Sid saying in response that she would probably plead crazy and be sent for a while to an institution and then be released in due time as all right again.

Which she did and was and probably will be.

We do hope that you have enjoyed reading this large print book.

Did you know that all of our titles are available for purchase?

We publish a wide range of high quality large print books including:
Romances, Mysteries, Classics
General Fiction
Non Fiction and Westerns

Special interest titles available in large print are:
The Little Oxford Dictionary
Music Book, Song Book
Hymn Book, Service Book

Also available from us courtesy of Oxford University Press:
Young Readers' Dictionary
(large print edition)
Young Readers' Thesaurus
(large print edition)

For further information or a free brochure, please contact us at:
Ulverscroft Large Print Books Ltd.,
The Green, Bradgate Road, Anstey,
Leicester, LE7 7FU, England.
Tel: (00 44) **0116 236 4325**
Fax: (00 44) **0116 234 0205**

THE DOPPELGÄNGER DEATHS

Edmund Glasby

While investigating a fatal car crash, Detective Inspector Vaughn's interest is piqued when forensic evidence points to murder, and he is shown the eerie antique doll found sitting on the passenger seat. The blood-spattered doll bears an extraordinary resemblance to the dead man, and on its lap is an envelope containing the message: 'One down. Five to go.' When a second doll is discovered beside another murder victim, the desperate race is then on to find and stop the killer from completing the set of six murders . . .

THE OTHER FRANK

Tony Gleeson

When Detective Frank Vandegraf hears of the unexpected death of his ex-wife, he travels to the tiny rural town of Easton to face the demons of his past. But it's no respite from the challenging urban crimes of his regular job. No sooner has he arrived than two bizarre, violent deaths occur, and he feels irresistibly drawn to help unravel a web of mystery and intrigue. However, he's out of his jurisdiction, obstructed by officials, and amidst folk hiding their own secrets . . .